THE
CIRCUS
LUNICUS

THE CIRCUS
LUNICUS

MARILYN SINGER

HENRY HOLT AND COMPANY
NEW YORK

Many thanks to Steve Aronson, David Lubar,
Roland Smith, and everybody at Holt

Henry Holt and Company, LLC
Publishers since 1866
115 West 18th Street
New York, New York 10011

Henry Holt is a registered trademark
of Henry Holt and Company, LLC

Published in Canada by Fitzhenry & Whiteside Ltd.,
195 Allstate Parkway, Markham, Ontario L3R 4T8.

Library of Congress Cataloging-in-Publication Data
Singer, Marilyn.
The Circus Lunicus / Marilyn Singer.
p.   cm.
Summary: Solly's stepmother forbids him to go to the Circus Lunicus, but gives
him an inflatable lizard that turns into his fairy godmother and teaches him
how to turn into a space lizard as well.
[1. Circus—Fiction. 2. Lizards—Fiction. 3. Mothers and sons—Fiction.
4. Humorous stories.] I. Title.
PZ7.S6172 Cj 2000   [Fic]—dc21   00-38873

ISBN 0-8050-6268-6
First Edition—2000
Printed in the United States of America on acid-free paper.∞
1   3   5   7   9   10   8   6   4   2

To Christy Ottaviano,
editor supreme

THE
CIRCUS
LUNICUS

CHAPTER 1

Well, boys, your dad and I are proud. Very, very proud," said Solly's stepmother, waving their report cards in the air. It wasn't hard for Solly to see she was talking to his stepbrothers, Jason and Mason. She sure wasn't talking to him. She pressed a button on the answering machine. "Boys, I'm very, very proud," came Solly's dad's voice. "I'm sorry I can't be there to tell you that in person. But things are so busy here in Boldwangia. Whoops, gotta go . . ."

Solly's stepmother smiled a starched smile. "He's going to put Boldwangia on the map!" she declared.

"Somebody ought to," said Jason. "It isn't there now."

"You mean he's nowhere?" said Mason.

"You boys are too funny," Solly's stepmother told them, though she didn't sound as if she thought they were. Solly certainly didn't. "Well, I guess I get to do the honors *all by myself*." She lifted up two big boxes from under the dining-room table. "Jason, for getting an A in science."

Jason grabbed the box and pulled out his prize quicker than a snake sucking out an egg. "Wow, a microscope! Just what I wanted!"

"Of course it is, dear," said Solly's stepmother. "And Mason, for being the best athlete in gym."

Mason ripped open his box faster than an anteater tearing apart a termite's nest, and pulled out his new basketball.

"Coolarama, Ma. Let's go shoot some hoops, Jason!" He ran out the door.

"Nah, I'm gonna study some nasal mucus—*boogers* to you"—Jason looked at Solly—"under my microscope." He hurried off to his room.

"Uh, what do I get?" asked Solly, chewing on his thumbnail. He wondered why he bothered to ask.

His stepmother blinked and stared at him as if she'd forgotten that he was there. She fiddled with the fake pearls at her neck. "Oh, yes, Solly. Well, I found something special for you. In honor of not flunking anything, you might as well have it now." She opened a drawer—the one where they kept

fuses, batteries, twine, and other assorted junk—
and pulled out something small and vaguely green,
then handed it to him.

Solly looked down at the gift. It was a lizard
made of some sort of rubber in a crumpled package
that was ripped at one corner.

"You put it in water and it grows," his stepmother explained.

"I know," said Solly. He had at least half a
dozen of those things—although none of them
were lizards. His dad hated lizards the way some
folks can't stand spiders or snakes.

"It looks like a lot of fun. I'm sure you'll want to
try it right out."

"Uh-huh. May I be excused?"

"Of course," said his stepmother. "Right after
you do the dishes."

"Of course," muttered Solly under his breath.

He shoved the lizard into his pocket and stuck
his tongue out at the sink.

★   ★   ★

"Someone's at the door," announced Solly's stepmother, not getting up from the sofa. "Will somebody get it?"

Neither Jason nor Mason got up, either. They
were too busy squabbling over the TV remote control.

"Hey, look, it's an ad for the Circus Lunicus," Jason said, having accidentally flipped to the local cable channel. The Circus Lunicus was a legend in Mintzville. There was a rumor that some of the performers were not from planet Earth. Everybody in town filled the stands, trying to figure out if the rumor was true. So far, no one had succeeded. Jason and Mason had never seen the circus. Neither had their mother. But Solly had.

For years the circus used to show up every June, regular as fireflies. And every June, Solly and his parents had gone to see it. All of the acts were wonderful. But Solly's favorite performer was the Ringmaster. The man was very tall and very thin and he had the strangest voice Solly had ever heard. Solly found him wonderful and terrible and for a long time he'd wanted to be just like him when he grew up. He'd never met the Ringmaster, but he could imitate his voice quite well—he'd always been an excellent mimic—and he did have the man's autograph. Nobody else he knew had one. It said, *To the Boy of Boys—There's no place like the circus!* It was signed, The Ringmaster.

The Boy of Boys ... it was what Solly's mom used to call him, and it was she who'd gotten him the prize. He never found out how. She was always doing things like that—surprising him with amazing treats: odd-looking stones, brilliant feathers, strange-tasting candy, crazy socks; but the autograph was by far his favorite. Even though he was too young to write script, he'd practiced tracing the signature over and over. Like a silly kid, or so he now thought, he'd planned to show his skill to the Ringmaster if they ever met.

Then suddenly, the circus stopped coming. Nobody knew why. There was a rumor that the Men in Black had deported the performers. But nobody really believed it. Solly missed them badly. That was the year he started missing so many things, the year his life completely changed. But now the circus was coming to town again. Solly wondered if perhaps his life would change again—for the better.

He stared eagerly at the picture of the Big Top on the TV. That was all there was to the ad—a photo of a tent with ticket and performance information scrolling over it. But still it gave Solly goose bumps.

"We're going opening night, right, Ma?" Jason declared.

"That's right," Solly's stepmother replied.

Yippee, said Solly to himself. It was just five days away.

"Pee-yip!" cheered Mason.

"Mason, you know I hate that kind of talk!" said his mother.

"Aw, Ma, it's just Backspeak," Mason told her. "All the kids talk like that."

"I don't," mumbled Solly.

Mason heard him. "All the *cool* kids."

The bell rang again.

"Will somebody pul-eeze get that door?" Everybody looked at Solly.

He sighed and went to open it.

Ruben, four months younger than Solly and twice his size, was standing there. He was Solly's best friend. More than a best friend, really, since once upon a time Solly had practically lived at his house. He'd be living there still if Old Staircase would let him get away with it. "We're your family now," she'd insisted when she and Solly's dad had married. She still said it sometimes, though Solly wondered who she was trying to convince—him or herself.

"Hey, Sollerella," Ruben greeted, waving something in a bag.

"Don't call me that."

"How's the wicked stepmother?"

"Shhh," said Solly. "She's got ears like a bat—except when *I'm* talking to *her*. Let's go to my room."

"So, wanna see what Grumpy sent me today?" Grumpy was what Ruben called his grandpa—although the name didn't fit. It fit *Solly's* grandpa, his dad's father, quite well indeed. His grandma, too, for that matter. As for Mom's parents, he'd never met them. Her mother died before Solly was born, and her father lived too far away. Solly didn't know where. His mom must've told him once, but he'd forgotten.

"Sure," Solly answered his friend.

Ruben pulled out a stiff leash and harness. He held them out and pretended he was walking a dog. "Invisi-pet!" he exclaimed. "No mess, no fuss, no bother!"

"Your gramps is nutty," said Solly. But he grinned when he said it. He'd met Ruben's grandpa only twice, but both times were memorable. Grumpy was a clown, a real one. He traveled even more than Solly's dad did on business, performing with circuses all over the world. But he'd never performed with the Circus Lunicus. "That bunch is too weird for me," he'd told Solly.

"You mean because they're aliens from outer space?" Solly'd asked.

"No. Because they're cheap," Grumpy had answered.

Solly laughed—but he didn't believe it. Not for a minute.

CHAPTER 2

Hey, maybe we could be in the Circus Lunicus with our thrilling acro-act," Ruben said. "Hoopla!" He threw his arms in the air. Then he lay down on the floor with his feet up in the air and his knees bent. "Hup, Solly!"

"Forget it," Solly said. "Last time we tried that you dropped me."

"I won't drop you this time. I've been working out on my dad's bench press."

Solly frowned. But he went over to Ruben and put his skinny stomach against Ruben's large feet.

"And now for the death-defying Wing-Dings!"

"Drop me again, and you'll be the one who's dead," Solly warned, grabbing Ruben's hands.

"Hup!" barked his friend, lifting his big legs and

little Solly high into the air. "Da-dada-da-da!" He hummed circus music. "Now, let go of my hands."

"I'm telling you, be careful," Solly said. Cautiously he released one hand, then the other. Ruben's legs quivered a little but didn't buckle. Then he started moving his feet around, slowly at first, then picking up speed so that Solly was spinning like a weather vane.

"Whee! Whoopee!" Ruben cheered.

"Ahhhhh," yelled Solly, scared but having fun.

Something fell out of his pocket, but he didn't notice.

"Okay, that's enough!" he shouted after a bit.

Ruben reversed speed until Solly was perched on his motionless legs again. Solly grabbed his hands once more until Ruben lowered him to the floor.

"That was great!" Ruben said.

"Hmmm, not bad," Solly agreed.

"Ha!" Ruben laughed at him. He rolled over. "What's this?" he said, picking up something from the carpet.

Solly peered at the green lizard. "Oh, that. My booby prize. From Old Staircase," he said, using his nickname for his stepmother.

"Hey, it's better than the shoe-polishing kit she gave you for your birthday—especially since all you wear are sneakers."

"Yeah, but Dad doesn't," Solly said. He mimed

shining his father's loafers, which Old Staircase had made him do—all ten pairs of them—before his father returned from a previous business trip.

Ruben laughed when Solly pretended to spit on and rub an imaginary spot that wouldn't come clean. Then Solly looked at the lizard again and shrugged. "You want it? You can have it."

"Yeah?" Ruben's parents didn't believe in giving him a lot of store-bought toys. Mostly they gave him books. "You mean it?"

"Sure."

"Thanks." He stuck the lizard in his shirt pocket. In its package, it was too large to fit and half of it stuck out. "Wanna do the act again?"

Solly knew he should say no. When something's perfect the first time, you don't try it a second time. But he'd felt pretty good whirling around like that, so he said, "Okay. Why not?"

And of course this time, just as he and Ruben were up to full speed, the door opened with a bang.

"Yikes!" Ruben yelled, startled. He jumped, his legs swayed, and Solly flew off, landing on the floor with a thump.

"What on earth is going on in here?" said Old Staircase.

Ruben didn't know what to say and Solly couldn't say anything. The wind was knocked out of him.

"Well, whatever is going on had better stop. Young man," she said to Ruben, "it's time for you to go home. Solly, it's time for you to scrub the bathtub."

"Uh . . . Jason . . . ," he managed to gasp.

"Jason's working on an important experiment."

"Uh . . . Mason . . ."

"Mason's practicing his slam dunk."

Solly sighed.

"See you tomorrow," Ruben said, heading for the door.

"Just a moment." Solly's stepmother reached out and plucked the lizard out of Ruben's pocket. "What's this? Since when are you a thief?"

"I'm not," Ruben declared. "Solly gave it to me."

Old Staircase stared at Solly with a peculiar expression, annoyed and smug. "You what?"

Uh-oh, Solly thought. If he lied, Ruben would hate him. If he didn't, who knew what his stepmother would add to his list of miseries? He bit at his pinky nail. "He's telling the truth. I gave it to him."

"You gave it away? Would you have done that if it was from Dorianna?"

At his mother's name, Solly stiffened. "You're not my mother," he mumbled.

Old Staircase's mouth tightened into a thin line.

"So you've told me . . . Well, you need to learn a lesson in the value of things . . ."

"Here it comes," Solly muttered. What would it be this time? Doing all of Jason or Mason's jobs for the next month? Well, he did those, anyway. Scrubbing the kitchen floor every day?

"Next week while Jason, Mason, and I go to the Circus Lunicus, you can stay here and clean your room."

"No!" Solly cried. Not go to the Circus Lunicus? No. He'd thought it would be bad, but not that bad. "I have to go to the circus. I have to!"

"The only thing you *have* to do, Solomon Yanish, is listen to me." She put the lizard on Solly's bed. "Now, as for you, good night, young man." She steered Ruben toward the door.

He turned and looked at Solly. "I'm sorry, Sollerella," he mouthed.

"I have to," Solly wept as the door closed. He picked up the lizard and flung it across the room. The already torn package split open, and the rubbery toy fell out.

Solly was too busy sobbing to see it flash a tiny green light, then wink out.

CHAPTER 3

The moon wouldn't let Solly sleep, it was so big and bright. "Isn't the moonlight terrible?" he said out loud. It was a line from some play his mother had been in. She'd been in a lot of plays. She was a wonderful actor. He didn't remember the particular one the moonlight line was from, except that she died in it. Then soon after she died in real life.

She hadn't been sick for very long, but to a five-year-old it seemed like forever. No one told Solly what was wrong. He knew his mom was babbling a lot, not making sense about things. The night she died he was over at Ruben's. His dad rushed in, gibbering something about how she was turning green. It scared Solly a lot. He was afraid Dad was sick, too. Carlos Ramirez, Ruben's father, calmed Dad down and they left together. Solly was half asleep when Carlos came back two days later and said gently, "I'm sorry, Solly. Your mother's gone." His father wouldn't talk about it—about her. He got rid of all her pictures, letters, scrapbooks, mementos. He wouldn't answer any of Solly's questions. Now Solly could only remember his mother in bits and pieces: a line from a play, a hand on his cheek, the coppery shine of her hair, the way she played connect the dots with the stars in the sky. But especially on a night like tonight, he still missed her a lot.

"I think I'll write to Dad," he said to the moon. He got out of bed, sat at his desk, pulled out some paper, and wrote, *Dear Dad, How are things in Boldwangia? Did you find any new markets for Ravon Cosmetics?* Solly scratched out the second sentence. He didn't care about makeup or where to sell it and he wasn't about to pretend that he did. He looked out the window again, then continued, *Is the moon full there tonight, too? Next time you go, take me with you. Ruben and I are practicing a circus act. It needs work. The Circus Lunicus is coming to town. Remember how Mom used to like it?*

Solly paused. That was another of his memories of her, one he remembered best: her excitement about the circus's arrival; her sulking when it left town, like a kid the day after Christmas. *Old Staircase* . . . Whoops, he thought, and crossed that out. *Casey won't let me go to the circus next week. Come home, please. Love, Solly.*

He read through the letter once. Would his dad get it out there in Boldwangia? Would he read it? Would it make a difference if he did? He folded the note into an envelope, addressed it, and stuck on a stamp from the couple he'd slipped out of Old Staircase's stamp box. Then, putting on his baggy jeans over his pajama bottoms, he sneaked out of his room and out the back door, hugging close to the house to avoid being seen.

The mailbox was down the street. At two in the morning, nobody was around. Dad liked to say they rolled up the sidewalks in Mintzville after ten. It wasn't an expression he made up, but he always said it like it was. Well, thought Solly, the sidewalks are still here. But the town certainly looked different. Prettier, with that silver moonlight touching everything. Mr. Harris's gravel driveway sparkled like a path of diamonds. Ms. Vitale's birdbath gleamed like a trophy. The moonlight made everything spookier, too, casting shadows where Solly had never seen shadows before. Anything could be hiding in them. Anything at all.

When Solly reached Ruben's house, which was as dark and quiet as everyone else's, he thought about throwing pebbles at his friend's window to wake him. But then he thought better of it. Soon he got to the mailbox.

He grabbed the handle and tried to open the slot. It was jammed. Oh, man, Nemo Blatz must be at it again. Nemo and his two pals, Ferd and Doug, were the town troublemakers. They did things like messing up the mailboxes and painting the stop signs so they said *Shop*. Solly sighed. He could try the mailbox on Loomis. But that was near the sheriff's house (which was why Nemo and his boys didn't usually touch it). Solly didn't want to run the risk of the sheriff, famous for being a light sleeper, seeing and reporting him to Old Staircase. They'd both want to know why mailing the letter couldn't wait until morning—and he wouldn't be able to explain to them that he just needed to send it *now*.

There was another mailbox Nemo and the boys wouldn't have wrecked. It was near the old fairgrounds. Hardly anybody used that box because Mrs. Perlofsky said once she tried to and a scaly green arm came out of the slot and grabbed her mail. The mailman told her she must've been eating too much of her fruitcake that night. He'd been collecting mail from that box for years and had never seen any kind of arms come out of it, let alone scaly green ones.

Solly told himself he wasn't afraid of scaly green arms—at least not much—and he set out for the mailbox. He walked quickly. Even though it was June, the night air was chilly. Moonlight swims were still several weeks away.

The houses got fewer. The cricket sounds got louder. Soon Solly heard other sounds too—strange sounds, like horses clopping, only deeper, heavier, and muffled music, like a pipe organ wrapped in blankets.

When he got near the fairgrounds, Solly stopped and took in a sharp breath. A cluster of wagons was gathered at the far end of the field. A procession was streaming from them, moving toward the midpoint. People, in all shapes and sizes, wrapped up in hooded robes, like a group of monks. And animals. Horses, as large as elephants. Elephants, as small as ponies. And something else. Something long and scuttling. Something that brought back the smell of sawdust, the feel of hard wooden bleachers, the sound of a piping calliope: alligators. Musical alligators, humming their way toward where the Big Top would soon stand.

Solly knew those alligators could mean only one thing—the Circus Lunicus had come to town.

CHAPTER 4

Fast and slow. Busy and lazy. Nothing and everything. Solly thought of opposites as he watched the Circus Lunicus set up. He had crept as close as he could to the crew, peering out from behind a wagon. The circus folk seemed to move two ways at once. So exactly, so furiously. Sometimes they seemed to be standing still, other times moving so quickly, they were a blur. It was weird. It was fascinating. Solly felt that he could watch them all night.

Once in a while someone would appear who seemed to walk or lift or carry like a normal person. But Solly couldn't see any of their faces because they never lowered their hoods.

He wanted to get a different, better view. Quiet

as a night crawler, he inched around the back of the wagon and scooted across to a second one. He didn't expect anyone to be behind there, so he was startled to see, a ways off in the field, someone standing in the moonlight. It was a small girl. She wore no hood, and she was walking around and around in a circle, looking up at the sky. Even above the sounds of canvas flapping and hammers tapping, of horses snorting and alligators humming reptilian tunes, Solly could tell she was crying. He wondered if he should try to talk to her.

"Bo-oy," drawled a man's voice close to Solly's ear.

"Yi!" he yelled, jumping into the air. Solly spun around. A tall hooded figure was standing next to him. He hadn't heard it approach at all.

"Quiet now," said the man. "We don't want to wa-ake the neighbors." The strange voice, with its odd habit of sometimes stretching out the middle of words, was soothing, scary, and unmistakable.

Solly swallowed hard. He wanted to run away. He also wanted to stay and listen to every word the man said. "I'm—um—sorry, Ringmaster," he stammered, brushing nervously at his hair. What do I say next? *I'm a big fan of yours, Ringmaster. I have your autograph, Ringmaster. Be my friend, Ringmaster.* No, that was stupid!

"You know how lo-ong you've been watching us, bo-oy?" the Ringmaster said.

"No, I don't," Solly answered honestly.

"Forty-seven minutes," said the man. "You have to pa-ay to watch the Circus Lunicus for forty-seven minutes, bo-oy."

"But, uh, you weren't performing," said Solly, amazed that he dared to contradict the man.

"Everything we do is a performance!" the Ringmaster declared, in a different, commanding voice. "That'll be two do-ollars and fifty-six cents."

"But I don't have two dollars and fifty-six cents," said Solly. "I don't have any money on me at all. See, I just came out to mail a letter . . . Oops, where is my letter?"

"There," said the man, shooting out a hand and pointing to the ground, where it had fallen out of Solly's pocket.

"Yikes!" Solly gasped. The hand was clawed and scaly. Solly grabbed the letter and backed away. But the man was faster. He clapped his hand on Solly's shoulder. And when Solly looked down at it, he saw that it was just an ordinary, if meaty, man's hand. Am I dreaming? Solly thought.

"You don't have two do-ollars and fifty-six cents, then you can do two do-ollars and fifty-six cents worth of wo-ork."

"Work? For you?" said Solly. The Ringmaster's

hand wasn't rough, but it was strong, and Solly didn't intend to argue. But he was surprised.

"Why not? You think circus wo-ork is beneath you?"

Instead of silencing him, the Ringmaster's slightly jeering tone made Solly's words gush out. "No! I *love* the circus. I used to go all the time with my parents. My mom—she got me your autograph a long time ago. I still have it. She never told me how she got it . . ."

"Your mo-other must be very persuasive," the Ringmaster said, this time sounding, what?— surprised, irritated, disturbed, amused, kind, all of the above? Solly wasn't sure. At any rate, Solly hadn't thought of his mother that way. "I guess she was," he said, wondering.

The Ringmaster didn't reply. He just led Solly away from the Big Top. "What do you want me to do?" Solly asked, confused. "Set up the poles? Unroll the canvas?"

"That's for the roustabouts to do-oo," said the man.

"Spread the sawdust? Feed the animals?"

The Ringmaster stopped midway in the field. "Here." From under his robe, he pulled out a small shovel.

"Here?" said Solly. "What do you want me to do here?"

"Dig wo-orms."

"Worms?"

"Yes. We use them for fo-ood."

"Oh," said Solly, wondering which of the animals ate worms. Not horses or elephants. Maybe it was the alligators . . .

"Start now," said the Ringmaster. "Wo-ork longer than forty-seven minutes and we will pa-ay you." He started to walk away.

"Uh, wait," Solly called.

"Yes?" The man turned back to him.

"What can I put them in?"

"This," said the Ringmaster, producing a bucket from one sleeve.

"Thanks," said Solly, taking it. The Ringmaster nodded and left. Solly set down the bucket and started digging.

The field was moist and rich. There were a lot of worms, and Solly knew how to find them. When he was small, he and his dad used to go fishing together. They never caught much, but it didn't seem to matter. For a long time after his mother was gone, his father didn't want to go anywhere. Then he met Old Staircase. She was a nurse. She took his blood pressure and then she took charge of his life. Now Solly's father never stayed home anymore. And he and Solly never went fishing.

Solly put in the last worm the bucket could hold

and stood, eager to reach the tents and see more of the circus up close. He wondered if the little girl was still there, and if so, was she still crying? But the Ringmaster was already in front of him, holding out his hand.

This time Solly managed not to yell in surprise.

"You did a good jo-ob," said the man, taking the bucket.

"I'm a good wormer," said Solly.

"You wo-orked eighty-nine minutes."

"I did?" It hadn't seemed that long.

"We will pa-ay you." The man handed Solly a small envelope.

"Hey, thanks!"

The man turned to go.

"I can come again tomorrow night and dig more worms, if you like," Solly said. It was the last thing he expected to say.

The Ringmaster didn't answer.

Solly watched him disappear in the shadow of the tents. Then he walked slowly toward the mailbox, deposited the letter, and headed home. It wasn't until he got near his house that he opened the envelope. In it was a small piece of paper that said, *Good for one free soda when you buy a ticket.* Solly stifled a laugh. Ruben's grandpa was right. The Circus Lunicus *was* cheap.

CHAPTER 5

It was nearly dawn by the time Solly got back to his house. School would be starting in just a few hours. The next-to-last day of school before summer vacation. Even though he wasn't a great student, Solly was sorry school was ending. He never had to deal with Old Staircase or her endless chores there.

With a sigh, he slipped through the back door into the kitchen. All that watching, worming, and walking had made him thirsty. He drank two big glasses of water, then poured a third and carried it carefully up to his room, where he set it on the night table. He was starting to unzip his jeans when a flashlight beam blinded him and someone doing a bad imitation of Old Staircase said, "And where have you been at this hour, young man?"

Startled, Solly flailed out with his hands and somehow managed not to trip. The beam left his face and lit up his visitor's eerily, under the chin. It was his stepbrother Jason. If he'd had a choice, Solly would've preferred Mason. He was strong and a bit of a bully. But Jason was sly and a snake.

"Getting a drink," Solly said.

"Really?" said Jason. "You usually put on your jeans to get a glass of water?"

"I was cold," Solly replied lamely.

"Yeah, sure." Jason played the flashlight over Solly's pants. The knees were dirty and damp. "Looks like you were digging a well."

"I was digging for worms," Solly said. He didn't have to say for whom.

"Yeah, sure," said Jason.

Before he could ask anything else, Solly said, "What are you doing in my room, anyway?"

"I thought you might want to be part of my next science experiment."

Solly winced. He'd been part of Jason's experiments before. Once Jason sprayed perfume on one of Solly's arms and furniture polish on the other, then stuck Solly in a tent and opened a jar of mosquitoes to see which arm got more bites. Another time he froze Solly's tongue with an ice cube and then made him see if he could taste three things: chocolate, lemons, and very rotten fish. The only reason Solly was willing to do the experiments was because Jason agreed to take over his job of feeding and cleaning the litter box for Old Staircase's cat, Frigate. Frigate was the only attack cat Solly had ever met—and the only person Frigate ever attacked was Solly.

"No, no more experiments," said Solly.

"Aww, why not?" asked Jason. He was walking around the room, picking up Solly's things and putting them back crooked or tipped or upside down.

"You know why not," said Solly.

"Well, then, I guess I'll have to quit my job of taking care of Frigate and give it back to you!"

"Oh, no. That wasn't our deal."

"It wasn't? Hmmm, I could've sworn it was. Well, if you don't want the job and I don't want the job, poor Frigate will just have to starve. And won't Mom be upset."

"Let her be," Solly muttered. There wasn't much more she could do to him.

"And if Mom's upset, she'll never change her mind about letting you go to the circus."

"She'll never change her mind, period," said

Solly. Old Staircase had never once given him a reprieve.

"She might be persuaded by her favorite son." Jason scooped something off the floor and dangled it from one hand.

"And which son would that be?" Solly said under his breath. Then louder, in Mason's husky voice, he ordered, "Hey, Ma, you're gonna let Solly go to the *cus-cir*, right?"

Solly's voice went up an octave. "The *cusser*? What kind of talk is that?" He bit off each word sharply the way Old Staircase did.

"Aww, Ma, it's just Backspeak," Solly rasped, Mason once again.

Jason let out a short, surprised laugh. If Solly could have seen his face at that moment, he would have noticed something resembling an amused respect. Then Jason shrugged. "Well, if you're not interested in a little fair exchange . . ." He turned to go.

"Hold it," Solly said, trying to keep the desperation out of his voice. "Okay. You talk to Casey and I'll do your experiment. What is it this time? Which gives me a worse rash, poison ivy or cracker crumbs in my pants? What makes me dizzier, being spun in the dryer or being swung back and forth fifty times by you and Mason?"

Jason grinned. "No, nothing like that. You're gonna like this experiment. You'll see."

"Well, come on, then, let's get it over with," said Solly.

"Not now," Jason told him. "Tomorrow night, when the moon is full."

"I thought it was full tonight."

"Almost, Solly, almost. But not quite. Tomorrow night. Okay?"

"Okay," Solly agreed.

"Good." Jason tossed what he'd been holding at Solly.

Solly almost ducked but caught it, anyway. It was that stupid lizard Old Staircase had given him.

"Tomorrow night," Jason repeated, slithering out of Solly's room.

Solly looked down at the lizard and sighed. "What a night," he said, plunking it into the glass of water by his bed. "What a night."

CHAPTER 6

They're here," whispered Ruben from his desk next to Solly's. Solly had been late for school today, so Ruben hadn't had a chance to talk to him on their usual morning walk. "Circus Lunicus is here."

"I know," Solly said, then yawned. It had been a rough morning. Old Staircase woke him—and that was something he always tried to avoid because of her *"and"* habit. "Wake up, Solly, *and* clean your room. Wake up, Solly, it's schooltime, *and* would you wash the bathtub when you come home ..." This morning it was, "Wake up, Solly, *and* make sure you do the wash later, *and*, for heaven's sakes, what's that ugly thing, *and* why did you put it here without a coaster ..." He barely had time to glance

31

over at the lizard—which had swelled to four times its size—in the glass on his night table before she was telling him, "Do that again, *and* you'll have to learn how to refinish furniture!"

"The Circus Lunicus!" Ruben repeated. "They're a few days early. Grumpy said they don't usually arrive till the day before they open."

"I know," Solly said once again, though he hadn't really remembered that.

Ruben didn't hear him. First of all, he was too excited by the news. Second, Sniffles Snellivitch was being so whiny, as usual, it was hard to hear anything above her noise.

"Well, I *thought* it was all right with Mom to take Piggy home for the summer, but last night she said I couldn't . . . ," Sniffles wailed as she glanced over at the class's pet guinea pig.

"This certainly is a problem . . ." Ms. Montrose, their teacher, was having a hard time getting a word in edgewise.

"I heard it on the radio this morning—they sneaked into town in the dead of night. Nobody saw them," Ruben went on.

"Somebody did," said Solly, but again Ruben didn't hear him.

"We're going to Iceland, you see . . . ," Sniffles bawled. "I mean, who goes to Iceland—nobody, right? But we're going for *three* weeks, so there'll be nobody to feed Piggy or clean his cage . . ."

"Class, is there anybody else who . . ." Ms. Montrose tried to cut in.

". . . or play with him or make sure he doesn't get eaten by a cat . . ."

"We have to go to the old fairgrounds right after school to see them," said Ruben.

"I don't know if that's a good idea . . . ," Solly said.

"Maybe we can show off our act . . ."

"Look, Ruben, there's something I've gotta tell you . . ."

"All right, all right, Sniff . . . I mean, Sheila," Ms. Montrose said. "I'm sure someone else can take Piggy."

"I mean, I know it needs a little more work," said Ruben, "but I'll bet some of the acrobats there could help us polish it . . ."

"Ruben, do you like digging in the dirt?" asked Solly.

"Someone, anyone?" begged Ms. Montrose.

"So, we'll do it, right?" Ruben said. "We'll go right after school."

Go ahead, Solly. Tell him now. Tell him you met the Ringmaster. Tell him what he was like. Hmmm, what *was* he like? Solly realized it was something he really wanted to know. "Sure, all right," he said to Ruben just as the room went dead quiet.

"Excellent!" exclaimed Ms. Montrose. "You're a real lifesaver, Solly." She picked up a bag from under the counter where Piggy's cage rested and plunked it on Solly's desk.

"Huh?" said Solly, staring up at her. "What's this?"

"Guinea pig food. You won't have to buy any for the whole summer."

"What would I want with guinea pig food?"

"Well, you wouldn't, but Piggy would," said Ms. Montrose, and the class laughed. "Now, I suggest you take home Piggy today to make sure he gets accustomed to your room. He will be staying in your room, right?"

Oh, boy. What just happened? was the first thing Solly thought. The second was, Old Staircase is gonna love this. "Yeah, I guess he'll be staying in my room," said Solly.

"Good. Take him home right after school."

"But he can't, Ms. Montrose," said Ruben. "After school we're—"

Solly shot him a look.

"You're what?" said Ms. Montrose.

"Worming," said Solly. "After school we're going to find worms."

"Well, I'm sure you can do that after you bring home Piggy," she said, raising one eyebrow. Then she turned to write something on the board.

"Worming? That's funny," whispered Ruben.

"Not as funny as you think," Solly replied.

CHAPTER 7

Solly was trying to tiptoe up to his room, which was hard to do because he was carrying a clunky guinea pig cage. If he could just get it in there without Old Staircase seeing him, he might be safe. His stepmother didn't come into his room often—mostly when she had to wake him, like this morning, and with school almost over, she wouldn't have to do that for months.

It turned out Old Staircase wasn't home, anyway. But Jason was.

"Aha! Is that a guinea pig I spy?" he exclaimed.

Solly nearly dropped the cage. "Don't do that, Jason!" he yelled. "Don't sneak up on me!"

"Hmmm, there's an experiment I've been meaning to try. I have everything I need for it except a guinea pig. . . ." Jason smiled a snaky smile. Solly wouldn't have been surprised to see his tongue flick in and out.

"You try any experiment on this guinea pig and I'll tell Dad what really happened to his swordfish trophy." Solly could handle being Jason's guinea pig, but he wasn't about to allow a real guinea pig to be the guinea pig. "I was just experimenting with the floatability of varnish." Solly mimicked Jason's "Who me?" voice and expression perfectly.

Jason's smile faded. It was one thing to hear Solly ape his mother and brother and quite another to be aped himself. He was also a little bit afraid of Solly's dad, and Solly knew it. "Your dad's in Boldwangia," Jason tried to sneer, but he sounded a little edgy.

"He won't be there forever," Solly said, and immediately he was sorry because Jason instantly snapped back, "You hope," and he smiled again.

"Creep," Solly muttered, pushing past him into his room.

"Don't forget tonight's experiment," Jason called after him.

"Don't forget to talk to your mother," Solly called back, but softly. He doubted that anyone could change her mind. Still, it was worth a try—and an arm, a leg, his hide, whatever Jason's experiment required this time. He kicked the door closed behind him and sighed.

There wasn't really room on his desk for the guinea pig, but Solly was in a hurry. He had to meet Ruben at his house in five minutes. I'll find a better place later, he thought, setting the cage next to a pile of books. Then he pulled off his backpack, heavy with guinea pig food, and tossed it on the bed—which gave him a glimpse of his night table and the lizard in the glass.

Holy ravioli! It had grown. It stuck out of the glass by a good six inches. Solly had never seen one of those things grow like that. Maybe it was some new, special kind. He wondered if it was going to grow even larger. But then wouldn't it need a bigger container?

There weren't any glasses in the house that large. Somewhere in the basement, though, there was an old metal bucket. That might do. He stuck his head out of his door. Jason seemed to be gone. Good. He didn't feel like any further conversations. He hurried downstairs.

The basement was neater than when he'd last seen it. Old Staircase had done some throwing away and straightening up. She actually liked cleaning up. When she had one of her organizing fits, it made it harder to find anything. Solly had to poke around awhile until at last he dug out the pail, wedged behind some bad paintings his stepmother did last year when she'd taken an art class. They were supposed to be pictures of Jason and Mason, but they looked like an elephant had sat on their faces. Even Dad refused to hang them in the living room.

Next to the paintings was a box he'd never seen before. It had his name on it. Even though he knew he'd be late to meet Ruben, he felt a sudden need to peek inside. He opened the lid quickly. His heart gave a lurch. There were his old stuffed turtle; a pale green sweater Mom had knitted for him; a dinosaur costume, also handmade; a jar of oddly colored rocks; and other things, all of which Solly remembered well but thought had disappeared long ago. His eyes felt watery as he lifted out a star map ("Here's Orion; here's Cassiopeia," he could hear her say). Underneath was something he'd never seen before: a sketchbook. On the cover, his mother's name, Dorianna, was written in eight different colors.

He flipped it open. The first sketch was a drawing of himself, a lot younger and rounder and sound asleep. It was quite good. The second drawing, his dad, also snoozing, in the hammock, was good, too. But the third picture was truly remarkable. It was a drawing of the Circus Lunicus, with the stands full of people; the clowns, the alligators, and the acrobats prancing around the ring; and there, in the center, the Ringmaster, welcoming the audience. Staring at it, Solly could almost swear the performers were moving. He shook his head in wonder. He'd had no idea that along with her other talents, his mom was such a fine artist. He wanted to look through the whole book, slowly. Then he remembered that Ruben was waiting.

Rubbing his eyes and tucking the sketchbook under his arm, he grabbed the bucket, raced upstairs, reluctantly thrust the book in his desk drawer, filled the bucket with water in the bathroom, and took it to his room. He picked up the glass from his night table and pulled out the lizard. It felt odd in his hands. Instead of smooth and rubbery, it was rough and almost scaly. How weird, he thought. It really *must* be some new brand. He put it carefully into the bucket and put the bucket, too big for the night table, next to his bed.

Then he raced over to Ruben's house.

★   ★   ★

"Some five minutes!" Ruben said.

"Sorry. I found ..." These drawings. By my mom, he was going to say. But the prize was too new.

"What?"

"Jason. Lurking."

"That skunk," said Ruben. "Anytime you want me to punch out his lights, let me know." As far as Solly knew, Ruben had never punched out anybody. This wasn't the first time he'd offered to deck Jason, though. Sometimes it was tempting to let him do it, but Solly didn't want his friend fighting his battles. Besides, then there'd be Mason to deal with. And Mason's b-ball friends. And last but not least, Old Staircase. Ruben certainly couldn't deck her.

"Thanks, but no thanks," said Solly.

Ruben shrugged, looking disappointed, as he always did when Solly turned him down.

He got over his disappointment quickly, as he always did, on the way to the old fairgrounds. "You have to remember to think light, light. Let me do the twirling. You just keep your balance and think light. That's the trick to being an acrobat. My gramps told me that."

"Yeah. Sure. Right," said Solly.

"When I tell 'em who my gramps is, I bet they'll be impressed. Grumpy's famous in circus circles . . ."

"Yeah. Sure. Right," said Solly again. He didn't really think the circus would want to see their act. Or if they did, they'd charge for their time. He meant to say all that to Ruben, but he didn't. He hadn't told him about last night's adventure, either. And he didn't know why.

"There they are, there they are!" Ruben sang out as he and Solly reached the fairgrounds. They could see the circus tents and wagons. Solly felt suddenly elated, as if he'd rounded a corner and run into an old friend.

Ruben raced toward them. Despite his own excitement, Solly, a slower runner, had a hard time keeping up with him.

When Solly reached him, he saw that his friend looked puzzled and upset. "There's nobody here," said Ruben, pointing to the Big Top's closed flaps and the shut doors of all the trailers. "Everything's closed up tight. Where are they all?"

"Maybe they're resting."

"All of them? Let's look around. You go that way. I'll go this way."

"Okay," Solly agreed. He walked around the wagons. One had a bright painting of an alligator on it. Another pictured a group of clowns. Then he came to one that showed a huge top hat. A pair of red Western boots were sticking out from beneath the wagon. Small boots, jiggling up and down. A chant seemed to accompany the movement. Solly couldn't quite make out the words.

Bending down, he peered at the boots' owner. It

was a little girl. She had large green eyes and red hair, and she was bouncing a doll on her knees. "Home," piped the doll, though it was the girl doing the talking. "I want to go home, home, home." Though he couldn't be sure, he thought she was the same kid he'd heard crying the night before.

"Hi!" he said.

She looked up at him, startled, slapped off his baseball cap, scrambled out the other side of the wagon, and ran away.

"Hey, wait!"

But the girl was already out of sight.

Solly stood up and frowned. The girl troubled him. She was none of his business, really. But she seemed so unhappy. Solly didn't like seeing kids unhappy. He bent down again to pick up his hat. It scuttled across the ground like a blue tortoise. "What the . . ."

"Back again, bo-oy," said a voice.

Solly whirled around. No one was there.

"Ringmaster! I . . . uh . . . where are you?"

"Right here," said the voice.

Solly looked about frantically. At last a small movement on the side of the wagon caught his eye. The top hat. There was an eye in the middle of it. A blinking, green eye, staring right at him.

Something nudged his foot. He looked down. It was his cap. Solly reached for it, and it flipped up onto his head. "How'd you do that?" he asked.

"At the Circus Lunicus, the eye is quicker than the ha-and," said the Ringmaster. "You want to learn my secrets, bo-oy? Is that why you're here?"

"Yes ... no ... My friend and I, uh, we have an act."

"What kind of an act? A clo-own act?"

"No," Solly said. "We're acrobats."

"We don't need more acrobats. But we always need clo-owns."

"We're not ... we don't want to ..."

"Everybody loves clo-owns."

"I know, but ..."

"Your mo-other loves clo-owns."

"My mother is dead!" Solly blurted.

The Ringmaster was silent for a moment. Then at last he said gently, "I'm sorry to hear you sa-ay that."

That's a strange way to put it, Solly thought, but then he figured the man must still be talking about clowns. "Clowns are great. And you're right—my mother loved them. But we're not clowns," Solly said, slowly and emphatically. "We're acrobats, and we don't want to join the circus." The last part wasn't true. Ruben would *love* to join the circus.

And Solly had thought about it many times himself. But it seemed like such an impossible dream.

"You don't?" said the Ringmaster. "Every bo-oy and girl wants to jo-oin the circus."

The man's tone bothered Solly. Was the Ringmaster mocking or coaxing him? Or something even more sinister? "*I* don't," Solly insisted.

The Ringmaster said nothing.

"Look, we just need some . . . help with our act."

"Yes, you co-ould use some help."

"You'll help us, then?" Solly said.

"I didn't sa-ay that. But come back after midnight, and we'll see."

"Tonight? I don't know if I can . . . I'm supposed to . . . I have to . . ."

"Tonight. And remember, we cha-arge by the hour," said the Ringmaster. Then the eye blinked and disappeared.

Solly went to find Ruben. His friend was sitting glumly on an overturned barrel. "Nobody. Nobody here at all," Ruben said. "Did you find anybody?"

"Well, sort of," said Solly.

"Sort of?"

"Uh, Ruben, you don't have any plans tonight after midnight, do you?"

"Are you kidding? Of course not."

"Well, you do now," Solly said, drawing himself

45

up so that for a moment he seemed as tall and thin as the Ringmaster. "And bo-oy, bring a bucket," he said.

Though he grinned at Ruben's startled expression, he wasn't sure whether the two of them should be thrilled or terrified.

CHAPTER 8

Solly was having a fight with his closet. Or rather with what was *in* his closet, which was most of his stuff. Not much more would fit in there, but Solly had to make room anyway to hide the small garbage can he'd found in the garage. Inside the trash can, floating in several gallons of water, was the rubber lizard. It had grown again.

How much bigger was this thing going to get? Would it break some sort of record, if there was a record for giant rubber lizards? From his cage, Piggy watched, unimpressed. But Solly scratched his head, nervous and fascinated.

The door to his room opened just as he managed to squeeze the can inside the closet and shut the door.

"What're you doing?" asked Jason, in a low voice. He was carrying something. It was shaped like a football helmet.

"Getting some clothes," said Solly.

"Get your earmuffs while you're at it."

"Earmuffs? Wait a minute, you're not going to pour ice cubes down my back again and see how long it takes to lower my temperature?"

"No." Jason smiled. "But that was a good experiment, wasn't it?"

"Good for nothing," muttered Solly.

Jason either didn't hear him or pretended not to.

"The earmuffs are downstairs in the hall closet," Solly said.

"Right, then. Let's go."

Solly didn't hesitate. He wasn't looking forward to this experiment, whatever it was, but he did want to get it over with. It was already eleven o'clock, and in an hour he had to meet Ruben under the apple tree in his backyard. Jason's experiments never took longer than an hour, so Solly thought he'd have plenty of time. The bigger problem would be sneaking out past his stepbrother when they were done.

Jason got the earmuffs from the hall closet and led Solly to the garage. "Okay, earmuffs on first," he said, handing them to Solly. Solly shrugged and did as he was told. "Now this." He passed the thing he'd been carrying to Solly. It *was* a football helmet, with something large and horseshoe shaped inside. A magnet.

"What is this for?" Solly asked loudly. "What is this experiment?"

"Shhh," said Jason.

Solly sighed and put on the helmet.

"Last but not least . . ." From his pocket, Jason pulled out a pair of dark glasses. He stuck them over Solly's eyes.

"Hey!" Solly cried. "I can hardly see!"

"Shhh!" Jason repeated, although Solly didn't hear him.

What he did hear was a faraway click, like a distant door opening. The next thing he knew he was sitting in a car. He felt it rumble awake.

"Jason, what's going on! Jason!" He clawed at his glasses.

Jason reached under his helmet and pulled the muff away from one ear. "Take those off and you'll be feeding Frigate for the rest of her life or yours," he hissed. "Now, sit back and relax. I'm a good driver."

"Good driver! You're only thirteen!"

He didn't hear Jason's reply.

They drove for what seemed like forever until, at

last, Jason stopped the car. Solly heard that faint click again and felt a rush of cool air, then Jason's hand on his arm as his stepbrother escorted him from the Chevrolet.

"Now, this is an experiment about the effect of magnets and the full moon on migration," Jason said, pulling aside one muff again and shouting. "I'm going to let you go and we'll see if without using your eyes and ears you can find your way home."

"You've got to be kidding!" said Solly.

"And don't touch the earmuffs or glasses—I'll be watching you the whole way."

"Jason, you've got to be kidding," Solly repeated. "Jason? Jason!"

But Jason was gone.

If the drive had taken forever, it was nothing compared to how long Solly had been wandering around who knew where. Ruben's going to kill me, he thought, turning left. It had to be way past midnight by now.

He took another left turn. I must be in some kind of big field, he thought, because I haven't bumped into anything yet.

He stretched out his hands. Nope, nothing. This experiment is nuts, he said to himself. What does Jason think I am, a pigeon? Then it hit him.

Pigeons are smarter than I am. They fly away from trouble. I let myself walk right into it.

He stopped dead, reached up, and tore off the dark glasses.

He had to blink only a few times to see where he was. In the moonlight the wagons seemed to glow, the Big Top to loom round and shiny as a flying saucer. "Welcome, bo-oy," a familiar voice greeted him. "You're right on time."

He had made it to the Circus Lunicus after all.

CHAPTER 9

The Big Top was tinged with a strange green gleam. Solly couldn't tell where the light was coming from. Gathered around the ring were a group of the circus performers. Tonight they weren't wearing robes. Solly could tell by their various outfits that some were acrobats, tightrope walkers, or trapeze artists; others were animal trainers; still others were jugglers, magicians, or clowns.

What he still couldn't make out well were their faces. He thought he could tell what they looked like and what expressions they wore, but every time he tried to focus on a face, it shifted and blurred, leaving just the impression of the person's appearance without any details. Even the Ringmaster was hard to see clearly. But Solly did have a better sense of *his* face—pleasant and oddly smooth, as if some-one had stretched a piece of thin plastic over it. Were they like that in the ring? Solly couldn't quite remember. It wasn't the faces he'd focused on then.

"Well, bo-oy," the Ringmaster said. "Sho-ow us your act."

"I can't," said Solly, shrugging with palms up.

The performers tittered.

"It's a two-person act, and my friend Ruben isn't here."

The performers laughed louder.

Solly's brow puckered. What was so funny?

"Sho-ow us your pa-art of the act," said the Ringmaster.

"Huh? I can't do that. I told you before—it's an acrobat act. Ruben lies down on the ground and I get on his feet and he lifts me in the air . . ."

"Show us," the Ringmaster insisted, clipping the words short.

Solly frowned. Was this guy nuts? But he leaned over and extended his arms, pretending that Ruben was about to hoist him in the air.

The Circus Lunicus roared with laughter.

Confused, Solly straightened up. His eyes caught a swift movement behind him. He spun around. One of the clowns was standing there, posed just like him. In a flash, Solly knew the clown had been mimicking his every move.

Annoyed, Solly turned back to the Ringmaster and the rest of the circus. "Ha, ha. Very funny," he said. Were they just mocking him?

"Yes. It was funny," said the Ringmaster. "Let's see some mo-ore."

"Forget it," said Solly, hands on hips. "I said I'm not a clown!"

The circus laughed. Solly whirled again to look at the clown. The clown whirled to look at Solly. "Cut it out!" said Solly. Cut it out, said the clown, using Solly's body language but not words.

Solly felt tears welling. Old Staircase, Jason, Mason—they were bad enough. Picking on him. Making him do any crummy job or experiment they wanted. But this ... Even with the Ringmaster's teasing and his mania for clowns, Solly had expected something different from the circus. Something magical. Something grand.

Shoving his hands in his pockets, he started to leave the ring. The circus was still laughing. He wished he could stuff cotton in his ears to block out the sound. Solly saw something move to his right. Probably that stupid clown again, he thought. He wanted to look straight ahead, but he cut his eyes there, anyway. It was the little girl. This time she didn't look frightened or sad. Instead she seemed curious. And *her* face—from the small freckled nose to the green eyes to the springy red hair that reminded him of his mom's—was totally clear.

Something surged up in Solly. All at once—and to his own surprise—he decided he wasn't going to leave. He wasn't going to let them *make* him leave. He whirled back to the Ringmaster. "You want to see more of my act?"

"Certainly," the man replied, and Solly could tell that he meant it.

Solly walked back to the center of the ring. Once again he pretended he was being lifted in the air. He spun one way, then the other. The audience howled. What next? he wondered, hoping he was making the girl laugh, too.

"Let me show you," said the clown, as if Solly had asked the question out loud. He demonstrated a few silly moves Solly could make. Now Solly began to imitate him. Soon he was cracking up along with the audience.

He turned to the Ringmaster. The man was leaning forward. He seemed to be studying Solly intently. Before, Solly had wanted to make the girl laugh. Now he wanted even more to hear the Ring-master's applause. "Well?" he asked.

"With practice, you just might make a very good clo-own," the Ringmaster conceded.

Solly grinned hugely.

"Now you pa-ay." The Ringmaster pulled out the bucket. "Fill it up."

"I should make you pay me," said Solly. "After all, this time *I* was the show."

The Ringmaster smiled. At least Solly thought he did. "You're learning, bo-oy. You're learning. We'll make it ha-alf a bucket."

Solly snorted. "Deal," he said. Then he had another thought. "But I'd like some company."

"Company?"

"Yes. That girl. That red-haired girl who's so homesick." He frowned. He hadn't meant to say that much.

"Ho-omesick?" said the Ringmaster. Then, in a loud announcer voice, he shouted, "No one is ho-omesick at the circus!"

Once again, Solly couldn't tell if the Ringmaster was taunting or cajoling him. What was the man's game? I should shut up, Solly thought. But instead, without knowing why it was so important to him, only that it *was*, he pressed, "Well, *she* is." He waited for the Ringmaster to ask him what business was it of his or just what he planned to do with this supposedly homesick kid. Instead the man asked, "And you, Bo-oy of Bo-oys. Are you ho-omesick, too?"

Solly gasped a little, hearing himself called that.

The Ringmaster must've remembered that autograph, how Solly's mother had made him address it. He wasn't sure he liked the way the man had said it. "Me, homesick? No. Of course not."

"You see," the Ringmaster said triumphantly.

"But why would I be . . . I'm home . . . I mean . . . I'm here . . . I mean, in Mintzville . . . ," Solly stammered. The Ringmaster had gotten him all confused.

"Ho-ome is where the art is."

"You mean the *heart*," Solly said, sure he hadn't heard right.

"That, too," said the Ringmaster, in such a matter-of-fact voice it made Solly smile.

Then he remembered the girl. "I still would like that girl's company," he said.

"Which girl?" asked the Ringmaster.

How many little red-haired girls could there be hanging around the circus? Solly nearly barked. Instead he turned to point her out. "That one . . . ," he began. But the girl was gone. And when he turned back, the Ringmaster was gone, too. In his place was a silver worm bucket. It was three times the size of the one Solly'd used last night. Half a bucket indeed! The Ringmaster had gotten him again.

CHAPTER 10

Where have you been?" Jason demanded in an angry whisper, grabbing Solly's arm and hauling him into his room. If Solly didn't know better, he would've said that his stepbrother was—or had been—really worried.

"What do you mean, where have I been?" Solly replied. "I was in the field where you left me, trying and trying to navigate home." He didn't mention his circus performance or the inscrutable Ringmaster, who made him feel twenty ways at once, or the red-haired girl, whom he'd thought about the whole way home. He knew *homesick* when he saw it, no matter what the Ringmaster said. For a second he let his face and body slump into the essence of the word until he looked just like the girl. Then he let the feeling go and wondered, Why was the man trying to fool him? What was the girl doing there? She didn't seem to *fit*. He wanted to talk to her and find out. But how?

"Field? What field?" Jason said. "I left you two blocks away in Hamlin Playground."

"Oh, sure," Solly retorted. "That's why it took forever to get there, huh?"

"I drove in circles so you wouldn't know where we were going."

"Cut the baloney," Solly said. "You left me at the old fairgrounds."

"I did not."

"You did too."

"I wouldn't do that—not even to you," Jason insisted. "Either my experiment's a failure, or you have the worst sense of direction in the world."

"I thought you were going to watch me the whole time. If you were watching, how'd I disappear from Hamlin Playground?"

"I don't know," Jason said. "One minute you were there; the next you were gone. I rode all over the neighborhood looking for you."

"And then you just gave up."

"I figured you were faking me out. That you'd taken off the helmet and the glasses and gone home. That was hours ago."

Solly opened his mouth, then closed it again.

Jason had told plenty of lies plenty of times. But Solly didn't think he was lying now. "I'm tired," he said with a sigh. "Go back to your own room and let me sleep. And don't forget to talk to Casey."

With surprising obedience, Jason started toward the door. Not even bothering to change into his pj's, Solly sank down on his bed and closed his eyes, waiting to hear the faint click that told him Jason had gone.

But then he heard his stepbrother ask, "So, did you see the circus? They're here, you know."

"No," Solly lied. "I didn't see them."

"Oh, really?" There was something shifty in Jason's tone, as if he not only didn't believe Solly but wondered why he'd be lying.

"It's a big field," Solly said.

"Not that big," said Jason.

Solly pulled the blanket up to his chin as if it would protect him from Jason's questions. He yawned again. "Good night, Jason," he said.

"You mean good morning. It's almost dawn."

In answer, Solly snored.

CHAPTER 11

It wasn't exactly what Solly would call a nice dream. High up in the Big Top, he and the red-haired girl were walking a tightrope, each coming from the opposite side. "You can do-oo it, bo-oy," a voice urged him on. Solly could hear the crowd cheering below, but he didn't dare look down. Neither did the girl. "I want my mama," she said, inching her way toward him. She was holding a bucket in one hand. Solly knew it was filled with worms. "I want my mama," Solly echoed her voice. "I don't want to fall," she whimpered. Solly reached for her hand. "Leave her alone, bo-oy," said the voice.

And then someone pushed him.

He yelled all the way down.

61

"Quit hollering," someone said.

Solly opened his eyes with a gasp. He wasn't dead. He wasn't even bruised. But all of a sudden he was suffocating. That was because Mason was sitting on his stomach.

"Get . . . off . . . ," he wheezed.

"Then stop yelling," said Mason.

Solly did, and Mason let him up for air. "Hurry up, squeak-pip. You're gonna be late for school."

Solly turned and looked at the clock. Twenty to nine. Oops. That made two days in a row he'd messed up. Old Staircase must be really annoyed. She sent the goon to get me, he thought.

"Okay, okay, I'm hurrying," Solly said, scrambling out of bed.

"Hey, you're already dressed," said Mason.

"No. These are my special pj's. They look like my regular clothes," Solly replied.

"Yeah. Right," said Mason. But Solly could tell that he wasn't sure whether or not to believe him. "Hurry up, will ya?" his stepbrother said, looking out the window. "Hey, Bodine!" He pushed it open farther and stuck his head out to talk to one of his b-ball pals. "What's the difference between a point guard and a puppy? None. They're both good dribblers. Haw, haw!"

Solly tripped over to the mirror hanging on his closet. Had he really performed for the circus last night? It felt as much like a dream as the dream he'd just had. He stared at his face and twitched his eyebrows up and down, then in a rippling wave. Mason was still yakking at the window, so Solly scrunched up his mouth till it was as pinched as Old Staircase's. He let it droop, and then he shivered with silent weeping. Slowly he turned the frown into a grin that got wider and more manic until he shook with equally silent laughter. Then he grinned and frowned for real. *What am I doing?* As he ran a hand through his bushy hair, he heard a rattle on the other side of the door. It sounded like something pushing at a garbage can lid. He put his hand on the doorknob.

"What are you doing?" Mason barked.

"Just clowning around," Solly muttered, dropping his hand.

"Well, quit it and let's go."

With a concerned glance at the closet, Solly turned and let his stepbrother shove him out of the room.

★   ★   ★

"Thanks a lot," Ruben hissed while Ms. Montrose scribbled *How I Will Not Spend My Summer Vacation* on the board.

"Today is the last day of school, and you're going to write your final essay," she was saying.

"But it's only a *half* day, Ms. Montrose. So we should write *half* an essay," said Sniffles.

"Ha, ha, ha." Ms. Montrose laughed, even though Sniffles was being serious.

"I'm sorry," Solly whispered back.

"Two hours. I waited two hours under the tree," Ruben sputtered.

"I know. I'm sorry," Solly repeated. "But it wasn't my fault."

"I want you to write about the things that you *don't* plan to do this summer. They can be things you'd like to do but can't, or things you'd hate to do and won't," Ms. Montrose went on.

"I don't know what I'm not doing this summer, Ms. Montrose," whined Sniffles Snellivitch.

"Use your imagination," the teacher told her.

"It was Jason," Solly said to Ruben.

"Yeah, well, when are you going to stop letting him bully you around?"

Solly shook his head cheerlessly.

"But Ms. Montrose, what if I imagine I'm not doing something and then it turns out I am?" Sniffles went on.

"Sniff . . . uh, Sheila, I don't think we have to worry about that," said the teacher.

Ruben wasn't someone who stayed angry long. "Okay. Then let's do it tonight."

Solly swallowed. He didn't know how to tell

Ruben he'd already shown their act to the Circus Lunicus and that it had turned into a solo, a clown act yet, which felt oddly *right*! How can a person feel both weird and, well, *comfortable* at the same time? he wondered. Yet that was how he felt doing his act at the circus. But it wasn't something he could tell Ruben.

Nor could he mention the red-haired girl, even though he couldn't stop thinking about her. Did she need his help? What could he do? Why was the Ringmaster being so cagey about her? Was the Ringmaster a good guy, a bad guy, or something else? How could Solly tell Ruben his feelings about that strange person when he wasn't sure of them himself? "I can't," he said.

"Why not?" Ruben demanded.

"Ruben, Solly, what are you planning *not* to do this summer?" Ms. Montrose asked sharply, looking at them both.

"It looks like I'm planning *not* to join the circus." Ruben scowled.

"Solly?"

"I don't know, Ms. Montrose," Solly replied. But he was thinking sadly, It looks like I'm planning *not* to have a best friend.

CHAPTER 12

Solly thought he was never going to get to his room. Old Staircase was waiting for him when he got home from school. She seemed in a worse mood than usual. She'd had a patient last night. She didn't have many of them anymore; the visiting nurse agency called her only when everyone else was booked up. "Casey doesn't have the patience for patients," Solly's father had said at dinner one night a year or so ago. Solly chortled along with him. Old Staircase got that pinched look, and later Solly'd heard her scold his dad for mocking her in front of the kids.

"The lawn," she commanded, blocking his way upstairs. "Mow it."

"Okay," Solly said. "Right after I——"

"*Now.*"

"Okay." He sighed.

The lawn took a long time because the power mower kept stalling and Solly had to use the antique push model his dad hadn't thrown away. And after that there was watering the flower boxes and weeding the vegetable garden out back.

When he finally finished, soggy and tired, Old Staircase smiled—actually smiled—at him. "Good job," she said.

He stared back at her, amazed she'd complimented him. "I was just telling Sheriff Selig what a hard worker you are," she said.

Sheriff Selig. Solly had no idea what the sheriff was doing in their house, but there he was, sitting in the kitchen.

"Sheriff Selig says someone thought he saw Jason last night. He says he was driving the car." She laughed. "I told him that was impossible. Isn't it, Solly?"

"Impossible," Solly said solemnly.

"Your car's license plate number is 62CGC, isn't it?"

"Yes. But it was in the garage. I walked to work."

"I saw it on the road last night. If Jason wasn't driving it, who was? Your other son, Mason?"

"Neither, Sheriff Selig, I assure you."

The sheriff stood up. "If I were you, ma'am, I'd have a talk with those boys of yours."

"Thank you for your advice," Old Staircase replied, smiling.

As soon as the sheriff was gone, the smile melted like rubber on a griddle. She whirled on Solly. "Just what do you think you were doing, driving my car?" she screeched.

Solly was stunned. "Me? I didn't ... I couldn't ..."

"You ungrateful boy. You have a nice house, nice clothes, a nice family, and you do this? Did you think you could get Jason or Mason in trouble? Just because they do better in school than you do? You're jealous, that's what you are. Jealous, jealous, jealous!"

Solly was too stunned to say anything. He began to gnaw at the nail on his ring finger.

"Your father will hear about this, mark my words. I'm calling him right now. It's the middle of the night in Boldwangia, so he might actually be in," she said with a sarcasm Solly rarely heard her use. "Hello, hello," she shrilled into the phone. Solly pictured his dad with his fingers in his ears. "... Oh, hello, Edmund. Emergency? I'll say it's an emergency. You must speak to your son. Right now. He was out joyriding last night. No, not Jason. No, not Mason. Solly! Yes, here he is."

Solly took the phone. "Hello, Dad," he said.

"Hello, son." His father's voice was hoarse with sleep. "What's this Casey's telling me about you driving the car?"

"No, Dad. I didn't . . . I couldn't . . ."

"Well, boys will be boys. Just don't do it again."

"But I . . ."

"What else is new?"

There was so much he wanted to say to his father. But Old Staircase was standing right there, and he suddenly couldn't remember all of it, anyway. "The Circus Lunicus is in town" was all that came out.

"Oh," he said tightly. "I hope you're not hanging around them. Circus people are not good role models."

Solly was stunned. Since his mother's death, his dad had changed. But Solly couldn't believe he'd changed so much that all he could say about the Circus Lunicus was that Solly should keep away from it. A new—or maybe a very old—anger rose in him. "Mom loved the circus," he said. "You remember Mom, don't you?"

"Of course I remember your mother," Solly's father answered with flustered seriousness. "You don't forget someone just because she disappeared . . . from your life."

Something was weird about what he'd said—or

69

how he'd said it. Solly wasn't sure which. But instead of making him more angry, it made Solly sad. "Dad, I miss you."

"I miss you, too, son," Solly's father answered, sounding distracted.

"Do you, Dad?" Solly whispered.

"Of course I do."

"Then when are you coming home?"

"Soon, soon. You know how it is with my business. You can't rush things."

"No, I don't know that," Solly murmured.

Then his father said, "Well, this call is costing a fortune. Why don't you put Casey back on?"

"Okay, Dad."

"And, son, stay away from Circus Lunicus."

In answer, Solly handed Old Staircase the phone and fled, at last, to his room.

Feeling as though his dad had sat on his heart, Solly rubbed his stinging eyes, which were threatening another bout of serious waterworks. He reached into his desk, took out his mother's sketchbook, and opened it right to the circus drawing. It really was a marvel—and wasn't that, there in the bleachers wearing a backward baseball cap, Solly himself? It made him smile. He began to leaf through the rest of the book. There were a few more circus pictures, but then came a different series of drawings. They showed a peculiar landscape Solly'd never seen before.

It was a swampy-looking place with a big moon shining down. Wait a minute, was that *two* moons? Or a *sun* and a moon? Solly couldn't tell. The first few pictures were mostly done in a realistic style, but then the style got wilder, with strange shapes and swirls of color, as if either the land was going crazy or the artist was. The very last drawing was just a big circle with arrows pointing toward a tiny word, written so small, Solly had to squint to read it. It said, *Home.* After that, the rest of the book was blank.

Solly felt a sudden chill. He knew, without anyone telling him, that those were his mom's last pictures, drawn when she'd been sick. His heart felt sore again, but it wasn't the same kind of pain. Tears rolled down his cheeks. He let them. Until he heard a noise coming from his closet. This time it wasn't a rattling. It was a small, spongy noise, like a balloon bobbing. Cautiously he opened the door.

The rubber lizard was standing there, its feet in the trash can, its head grazing the top shelf. It looked at Solly with yellow eyes. "Freeble, freeble, freeble," it said.

With a squawk, Solly staggered backward. Then he passed out cold on his bedroom floor.

CHAPTER 13

When he came to a few minutes (a few hours?) later, the lizard was still there, standing in the middle of the room and freebling more urgently than before. Rubbing its stomach, the creature curled back its green lips to reveal small but sharp-looking teeth.

Whimpering, Solly scuttled beneath the window and wondered if he could jump out. Another wave of light-headedness washed over him, but he was determined not to faint again. He took a deep breath and slapped his cheeks vigorously. It helped jump-start his brain. *If it wanted to kill you, it would've done so already,* he reasoned. *Unless, of course, it only kills moving prey . . .*

"FREEEEBLE!" the lizard said. *Whined,* Solly

thought. Then the reptile's belly let out an enormous rumble. "Freeble," it repeated, with a pleading look in its yellow eyes.

Solly took another deep breath. "Hungry?" he guessed, with a croak.

"Freeble." The lizard nodded.

Realizing that the six-foot-tall monster was famished should have scared Solly even more. But somehow, it didn't. There was something about the creature that suddenly reminded him of a toddler desperately in need of a feeding.

Solly glanced around his room. There was a bag of trail mix in his underwear drawer. He always kept one there in case of emergencies. Cautiously he rose and made his way to the bureau. He dug out the bag. His hand shook as he offered it to the lizard.

But the reptile turned up its nostrils. "Freeble," it sneered.

Okay, so nuts and dried fruit wasn't its thing. What did lizards eat? Ruben once had an iguana. It ate leaves. Solly went over to his window. A climbing rose his mother had planted years ago grew nearby. He was sure rose leaves weren't poisonous. He reached out as far as he could and managed to snare a few of them. He laid them on his desk.

But the lizard didn't want those, either. "Freeeeeble," it quavered, staring at a corner of the room.

Solly followed its gaze. It was focused right at Piggy, resting peacefully in his cage.

"Not on your life!" Solly snapped. No lizard, six feet tall and sharp toothed or not, was going to chow down on a helpless guinea pig in *his* house. He hurried over, lifted Piggy out, and held the rodent tightly against his chest. The guinea pig squealed and nipped his finger. "Ow!" Solly yelled, nearly dropping him.

The lizard didn't seem to notice. It was still looking at the cage. There was a large lettuce leaf lying on the bottom.

"Oh, maybe you like *those* kind of leaves," Solly said, depositing Piggy back in the cage and taking out the lettuce.

He held it out to the lizard, this time managing to keep his hand steady. The creature's eyes gleamed. It reached out a claw, turned over the leaf, speared a pale worm from the underside, and swallowed it.

"Sneeble," it said, with what Solly was sure was a smile. Then it searched the leaf again and again and frowned. "Freeeble, moreeeable!" it whined, its eyes getting that pleading look again.

"Oh, no." Solly sighed. He knew what that look meant. It meant he was about to go worming for the third time that week.

CHAPTER 14

The lizard finished the last worm (a caterpillar, actually). Solly had discovered that the fat chartreuse ones on Old Staircase's tomato plants were really its favorites.

His stepmother was surprised and even pleased at Solly's voluntary garden pest removal service, which included their own and several of the neighbors' yards. Over the past day and a half Solly had left the lizard alone *only* to go bug picking or to bolt down a meal himself. First he was nervous about what trouble the creature might get into. But the lizard was remarkably docile. It slept, hummed, and talked quietly to itself, complaining only when it was hungry. It seemed to be growing some more—not bigger or taller, but *older*. Its speech was clearer, its movements surer. It wasn't Ruben, but it was better company than Jason or Mason. Solly was beginning not to mind it as a roommate—but he worried about what trouble *he'd* be in if anyone found out.

"All goneeable?" said the lizard, looking into the bucket.

"All goneeable," Solly replied.

It sighed and let out a loud, aromatic burp. "PU," said Solly, although the burp didn't really stink—it smelled more like the color green, if it had an odor.

"Good sneeble," the lizard said, patting its stomach. Then it yawned. "Now sleeble." It closed its eyes.

"SOLLY, DINNER!" Old Staircase hollered from the foot of the stairs.

"Uh . . . okay," he yelled back. Then to the lizard he said, "You can't sleep here. Get into the closet—and stay there till I come back."

With another yawn, the lizard trundled into the closet like a sleep-walking kid.

Solly shut the door and nervously went down to the kitchen.

Old Staircase was an erratic cook. Some nights she made fabulous meals. Other times her dinners were on the strange side—pasta with radishes, sardines with raisins. Maybe that was where Jason got his interest in science. His mother's meals sometimes resembled chemistry experiments.

Tonight's dinner looked normal, even good—tacos with salsa. Last night he'd eaten a quick sandwich, using the excuse that he was tired. Tonight, if he didn't stay and eat the whole meal, Old Staircase would notice and demand an explanation, which was the last thing he wanted to give her. He decided to shovel in the food as quickly as he could and leave so he could get back to Freeble.

Jason and Mason were already at the table. They were gobbling their food, too.

Old Staircase didn't seem to be paying attention. She was thinking about something.

"The circus opens tomorrow," Jason said calmly, but Solly could tell he was excited.

"The midway opens *tonight*," Mason boomed. "I'm gonna go win me one of those stuffed alligators and laugh at the *keystur* waiting on line for tickets they're never gonna get."

Old Staircase was too preoccupied to criticize his Backspeak. "I've decided that I need a new hobby," she said, focusing on Solly, who'd made the mistake of looking back at her.

"Ummph," said Solly through a mouthful of taco.

"I hear that five fights broke out on the

ticket line already this afternoon—and the box office wasn't even open." Mason laughed gleefully.

"Painting was too . . . limiting. I need something where I can *really* express myself." Old Staircase continued to speak to Solly.

"Mom," said Jason casually. "You are going to let Solly go to the circus after all, aren't you?"

"Fumph," said Solly, suspecting Jason had deliberately chosen the wrong time to keep his end of the bargain.

Old Staircase ignored him. "Something like scuba diving . . ."

"He's sorry for whatever jerky thing he did," Jason continued.

"Or . . . acting. Yes, that's it. I've always wanted to act. I think I'd be good at acting, don't you?"

"Gack." Solly nearly choked. His parents had met when his dad saw his mom play Juliet. "Radiant," said both Solly's dad and the reviews. He became her real-life Romeo, attending every performance, appearing backstage with chocolates (which she didn't like) and roses (which she adored). They got married two months later.

"Wonder how many fights there'll be tonight," said Mason.

"He's learned his lesson . . . ," Jason went on.

"You don't think I'd be a good actress?" Old

Staircase frowned at Solly and fiddled with her necklace.

Say yes, sure, fine, he told himself. *Home is where the art is,* he could hear the Ringmaster say. "Not really," he mumbled into the salsa.

Old Staircase stiffened.

"So let him come with us," Jason finished.

She snapped her neck at him. "What are you going on about? No, Solly hasn't learned his lesson and he's not going to the circus."

"Well, then, give me his ticket and I'll sell it. It's worth a small fortune," Jason rapped back, holding out his hand.

Then they heard something thumping above their heads.

"What on earth was that?" asked Old Staircase.

"Uh ... I ... Frigate ... litter box ... needs changing ... ," Solly stammered, jumping up.

"Well, go take care of it," said Old Staircase. She seemed unaware that the sound was coming from Solly's bedroom, where Frigate never went. "And don't forget to do the dishes afterward. I'm going to a movie with Carla Walters."

"I will ... I won't," Solly called, racing out of the room.

He ran into Frigate on the stairs. She hissed and swiped a paw at him. "I wish *you'd* take up scuba diving," he hissed back, then flung open the door to his room.

The lizard had gotten out of his closet and was sitting at his desk—or more precisely, at his computer—with Piggy in its lap, stamping its feet on the floor in utter delight. It was playing Planet Nine from Outer Space, Solly's toughest action game. And it was winning.

CHAPTER 15

How on earth do you know how to play that?" Solly asked.

The lizard squinted as though it was about to answer. But then it just shrugged. Smacking its lips, it cocked its head. "Sneeble," it said plaintively.

"Too bad. You've just had sneeble. And even if you hadn't, I can't go worming right now."

The lizard shrugged again as if to say, "Well, you can't blame me for trying." Then it stood up, put Piggy back in his cage, and patted the chair.

It took Solly a moment to realize that Freeble, as he was beginning to call the lizard, wanted him to sit at the computer. "Why?" he asked.

Freeble nodded at the screen and patted the seat again.

"You want me to play? All right." With a sigh, Solly decided to humor it. He sat down, took hold of the mouse, and double-clicked. The voice of Zyphoid, the game's villain, blustered from the rather tinny speakers. "So, you think you can drive me and my minions from Planet Nine? Go ahead, fool, and try!" and the first alien—a snot-dripping mongoose with a weapon resembling a Hula-Hoop—appeared on the screen.

Solly wasn't a bad player, but he wasn't a great one, either. Freeble stood watching as he made it through level three, then got zapped by something that looked like a boil-covered tomato.

"Zaleeble," Freeble said, gesturing to the screen.

"Huh? You want me to play again? What for? I mean, this is very *pleasant* . . . ," Solly said, wincing when he realized that he was using one of Old Staircase's favorite words and, besides, it wasn't particularly pleasant having an immense reptile of unknown origin in your bedroom, watching you get slimed by tomato guts. "But I don't think I feel like . . ."

"Zaleeble!" Freeble commanded. Not threateningly, not nastily, but forcefully enough for Solly to call up old Zyphoid once again.

The first three levels went fine, just as before. Solly braced himself for Tom-Ate-O. When it appeared, he felt Freeble's hands on his shoulders. If he hadn't been so into the game, he might have shaken them off. But he was too busy trying to evade the evil red fruit. And besides, the lizard's hands were cool, soothingly cool, like salve on a sunburn, but with some sort of pulse of energy.

Suddenly Solly's own hands felt . . . intelligent. Splodge! Tom-Ate-O exploded under Solly's barrage of boil-busting hornworms. He downed ten more aliens in quick succession and moved up level after level until he was on number nine.

"Whoo-ee! Yahoo!" he yelled as Zyphoid himself appeared.

"So, we meet at last," said the archvillain, which was true—Solly'd never gotten anywhere near level nine before. Jason, whose hand-me-down game and computer these were, had told him he never would. "Well, Jase the Lowercase, look at me now!" Solly roared, easily deflecting Zyphoid's slew of Death Dung Meteors.

"This fight has just begun!" Zyphoid declared.

"Ha! That's what you think!" exclaimed Solly.

Then he made the mistake of looking down at his hands.

They were green and scaly.

Solly screamed and jumped up.

"Got you!" Zyphoid intoned as the on-screen Solly got crushed by a snake-writhing asteroid.

"What have you done to me?" Solly yelled.

83

"Yeseeble! Good changeeble! Learn fasteeble!" Freeble babbled excitedly. Was it angry or elated? Solly didn't know, and he was too frightened to care.

"Help me! Give me back my hands!" he cried.

"Canteeble." Freeble shook its head. "Youweeble." He pointed at Solly.

"Give them back!"

"Canteeble," the lizard repeated, moving toward the closet.

"No! Where are you going?"

Freeble walked into the closet. "Youweeble," it said softly but firmly, then shut the door.

"Open up! Open up now!" Solly yelled. He was afraid to try pulling the handle, afraid to look down and find out what his hands could or couldn't do.

"Anything you say," said Jason, barging into the room.

Solly shrieked and sat down heavily on the floor, managing as he did to shove his hands under his butt. He hadn't heard his stepbrother come down the hall.

"What's going on in here?"

"N-nothing," Solly stammered, trying to keep his eyes on Jason and away from the closet.

"Pretty loud nothing ... Ruben's not here, is he?"

"No. Y-you know he's not."

"Haven't seen him around in a while. You didn't have a fight with him or something?" Jason asked.

"Or something," Solly replied. Normally he wouldn't have encouraged this line of questioning, but if it would keep Jason's mind off the closet and what was in it . . .

"Well, never mind. The guy's a loser, anyway."

"What does that make me?" Solly muttered.

Jason didn't answer. Instead he asked, "Something wrong with your legs?"

"My legs? Nope. My legs are fine. Just fine," Solly answered. He felt a geyser of nervous giggles threatening to erupt out of his throat and tried to hold it down.

"Then get up. You look jerky sitting there like that."

"I like looking jerky," Solly said.

Jason raised an eyebrow. "Maybe you should put that on a T-shirt and wear it," he said, and he turned toward the door.

That was it? That was *all*? Jason was going to leave him alone? Wasn't going to fling open the closet door? Wouldn't bother to get to the bottom of the disturbance?

Jason put his hand on the doorknob. Solly shifted on the floor. His wrists were aching from the way they were bent beneath him. One more moment and he'd have to shake out his hands—his green, scaly hands. Solly shuddered.

Then Jason whirled, dashed to the corner, and threw open the closet door.

In less than a second, Solly jumped up and flung himself on his stepbrother's back.

"Oof." Jason's breath whooshed out. Solly tossed him aside as though he were a paper cup and kicked the closet door closed. If that startled his stepbrother, it startled Solly more.

Jason lunged at the door again, and once more Solly shoved him away. But not before his stepbrother got a glimpse of his hands.

"Wow!" Jason said.

"Get away from me! Get away!" Solly yelled. He tried to push him a third time. But Jason seized Solly's wrists and held up his hands.

His pink, calloused hands with the bitten nails.

"What did you do with them? What did you do with those cool gloves?" Jason demanded, patting Solly's pockets, scanning the floor.

"Nothing. I did nothing!" Solly shouted. With a sob, he ran out of the room. He didn't even care that he left Jason—and Freeble—behind.

CHAPTER 16

Solly ran hard and fast, as though he could leave his skin behind him. He had to see the Ringmaster. If anybody could help him, the Ringmaster could. He knew how to handle alligators, and alligators were just big lizards, weren't they? Never mind that no normal alligator could make your arms turn green and scaly . . . Don't go there, Solly, he warned his panicked brain, and ran faster.

It was just getting dark when he got to the fairgrounds. He stopped dead near the newly erected ticket booth. He'd counted on the place being deserted of anyone but circus folk, and he'd counted wrong.

TOMORROW IS OPENING NIGHT said a big green-and-yellow sign over the booth, where a long line of foolish people who hadn't already bought their tickets were squabbling over the remaining few. Other Mintzville residents were milling around the grounds, hoping to get a glimpse of the performers or buying funnel cakes and alligator-shaped ice pops from the stalls already open for business.

The game booths, such as Squirt the Earthling, Toss the Moon, and Whack-a-Martian, were also in operation. There was a commotion at the latter. Nemo Blatz and his pals had pulled the mallets out of their holders and were whacking the people around them instead of the mechanical critters. Apparently they'd just picked on the wrong victims: Mason and a couple of his buddies.

"Crap!" Solly swore, darting in the opposite direction—right into Ruben and his dad.

"Solly!" hailed Carlos Ramirez. He was a big, shaggy man with a broad, toothy smile. In his right hand, he carried a puff of spun sugar that glowed like a bouquet of roses in the waning light. With his mane of hair and his furry arms, he reminded Solly of Beauty's Beast from the fairy tale. Solly shuddered and looked down at his own arms. They were smooth and nearly as pink as the cotton candy. "Fancy meeting you here!" said Carlos.

"Yeah, just fancy," Ruben muttered, staring at Solly.

Solly scuffed his feet and didn't reply.

"Isn't this fabulondo?" Carlos boomed, waving his cotton candy. He was always inventing words.

Usually that would amuse Solly. But not tonight. "Great," he said distractedly, wondering how to make his escape.

"I can't *wait* to see the show, can you?"

"Can't wait," Solly said flatly. Out of the corner of his eye, he saw Ruben's expression soften. His friend knew about Old Staircase's punishment.

Mr. Ramirez squinted and cocked his head. "How's your dad, Solly? Hear from him lately?"

Solly cleared his throat edgily. "He's fine. I talked to him last night."

"That was *kind* of him. When the hell is he coming home? A father's supposed to be with his son!" Carlos growled. He was angry at Solly's dad and he didn't try to hide it. The two men had had a falling-out over Old Staircase. Carlos had said she and Solly's father were as bad a match as a jackrabbit and a Jack Russell terrier. He wasn't invited to the wedding. Maybe losing your best friend ran in the family.

Soon. He's coming home soon, Solly was going to say. It was what he always said when anyone asked. But this time he didn't feel like it. "I don't know when he's coming home," he said truthfully.

"Neither does he," said Carlos.

Solly bit his lip. Now *he* was getting angry, but at

89

whom? His own father or Ruben's for bringing up the subject? He needed to get away. He'd nearly forgotten why he was there. "I've got to . . ."

". . . go get Grumpy," Ruben said at the same time.

"Grumpy's coming?" Solly asked, startled. Ruben must've been even madder than Solly thought not to have told him before.

"Yeah. He's flying in tonight," Ruben said, a little sheepishly. "Do you want to come with us to pick him up?"

It was his way of making up, and Solly knew it. He wanted to say yes. But he just couldn't. It was a long ride to the airport. He wouldn't be back for hours, and he had to see the Ringmaster as soon as he could.

"I can't," he said.

"Why not?" Ruben asked.

"I—I mean, I'd really like to, but I've got some chores to do," he stammered.

Ruben's lips tightened. "Yeah, right."

"I have to straighten up my room . . . ," Solly went on, knowing he shouldn't.

"Skip it, Solly," Ruben said. "Let's go, Dad." He walked away.

But Carlos gazed down at Solly. "I didn't mean to upset you before, about your dad. He's never been the same since your mom disappeared . . . from his life."

Click. That weird mushy phrase. Just like his dad had used. Had they always talked that way? He'd never noticed. But he did now—and it bugged him. "You mean since she *died*," he snapped.

"That's right. Since she died," Carlos said, looking down at the ground.

"Dad, let's go!" Ruben called from a few yards away.

"Take care of yourself, Solly," said Carlos. He gave Solly a squeeze on the shoulder and strode toward his son.

Solly stood there, watching their retreating backs. He hadn't talked much about his mom's death with Carlos. It was the one subject Ruben's normally forthright dad always seemed uncomfortable about. Solly noticed that a lot of grown-ups were uneasy discussing death. However, he'd never suspected Carlos of lying to him. But he was certain he was lying now. And that scared him even more than having green scaly arms.

He nearly ran after them to find out what was going on. But it was too late. Mason and his friends were swaggering toward him. Mason had one of the mallets, and he was beating on his own chest like a demented ape. He and Solly saw each other at the same time. With a Tarzan yodel, Mason charged.

Solly hurtled past him, quick as a monkey. He knew his stepbrother was just goofing around. But Mason playing was just as dangerous as Mason fighting. He plunged into the milling crowd. He didn't know whether his stepbrother was following, and he didn't want to take the time to find out. But where was he going? The Big Top was too conspicuous—and too far.

He heard the yodel again. If Mason caught him now, he'd have him on a leash like a pet dog (maybe even a *real* leash—he'd done it once before), or worse, he'd drag him home. Either way, Solly wouldn't get to see the Ringmaster at all.

Desperate, Solly swung toward the wagons. They gleamed dimly in the last moments of twilight. He flew past the ones with the alligators, the acrobats, the clowns painted on their sides. "Where is it, where is it," he wheezed, searching wildly. There! The top hat seemed to rise from the wagon and float toward him.

"Please, please, please," Solly huffed, barreling up the short flight of steps. The door was unlocked. "Oh, thank you!" he exhaled. He flung it open, hurled himself inside, and slid down to the floor, shaking and panting.

It was dark and close in the wagon. At first Solly

could barely catch his breath. He expected to hear Mason's Tarzan yell any moment. But there was no sound except a low mechanical humming. Eventually he started to breathe more slowly and deeply.

The place had a funny smell—kind of swampy. But it wasn't unpleasant. He wondered when it would be safe to leave. He wondered what he was doing here. He wondered what his mother would think if she could see him now, hiding in the Ringmaster's wagon, if she hadn't disappeared from his life.

Click. *Disappeared.* The word echoed in his head. *Dis-ap-peared.* "Your mother's gone" was what Carlos had said that night. Gone, but not forgotten. Gone, but not . . . *dead.* What if she was alive! He began to breathe faster again. He forced himself to slow down. No, she isn't, Solly. You know she was sick. You saw her. And there was a funeral, wasn't there? But he hadn't gone to it. Dad had said he was too little, and it was better to remember Mom when she was alive and beautiful. And she had been beautiful, with those green eyes and red hair . . .

Solly was going to cry again. His eyes felt as swampy as the air in the wagon. Then he froze. There was a noise behind him, behind the door. Hadn't he locked it?

He scuttled forward, feeling his way to some kind of chair, and crawled beneath it.

The door opened. A small shadow slipped into the room. It seemed to pause and look around, then move toward the opposite wall. Solly strained his eyes to see.

The mechanical humming got louder. Suddenly the wall lit up. It wasn't a wall at all. It was a console. It looked like the control panel of an airplane.

Or perhaps a spaceship.

CHAPTER 17

The lights were flashing and bleeping. They'd been doing that for a solid minute. From under the chair, Solly could figure out their pattern: 1, 3-3, 4, 2-2, 5, 9-9-9. But he couldn't see who was pushing the buttons. He crept forward a little. Now he could just make out an elbow.

Then all of a sudden a crazy flash of green light zipped across the room, blinding him, and a high-pitched whine drilled into his brain. He stuck his fingers into his ears, but it didn't help.

"Stop it!" he yelled, or thought he did. He wasn't sure he'd actually made a sound—or if he had, that anyone could have possibly heard it.

After what seemed an eternity the noise stopped

and was replaced by a different whine: "I told you, I want to go home! I hate it here! Take me home!"

"Serena, you *are* ho-ome. Wherever we are is ho-ome."

Solly blinked rapidly. His vision was returning. But he didn't need it to identify the two speakers. He knew perfectly well who they were.

"No, it's not!" sniveled the red-haired girl—Serena, Solly now knew her name.

"You are no-ot being re-easonable," the Ringmaster told her. His voice was low and he was stretching out his words even more than usual. Solly's mother used to speak slower, too, when he'd misbehaved once too often.

Solly felt a sudden sympathy for the man. Maybe there was some sensible explanation.

"You sa-aid you wa-anted . . . ," the Ringmaster went on.

"I want to go HOME!" Serena bawled, cutting him off. "I want to see Mommy!"

"I'm afraid you ca-an't. You ca-an't go ho-ome."

Serena began to bawl.

The Ringmaster sighed. "You pro-omised me you wouldn't act this wa-ay. I have no choi-oice now. You're going to have to sta-ay with the croco-dilians."

The crocodilians? Any trace of sympathy Solly

had for the Ringmaster disappeared, along with all trust. He was going to lock up Serena with the alligators, Solly realized with horror, as the girl's sobs rocked the wagon. The man was a monster! What should I do? Solly thought frantically. Wait till they leave, then call the cops? Follow them, and when the Ringmaster's gone, unlock the cage . . . or wagon . . . or wherever Serena would be kept?

He swallowed hard and choked on some dust from the floor. It tasted like dried pond scum. He couldn't help coughing.

"Bo-oy, come out from under that cha-air," the Ringmaster commanded.

Solly gasped and wheezed some more.

"Bo-oy, don't ma-ake me order you again."

Slowly Solly crawled out from under the chair. He stood up, facing the Ringmaster. The man was in his robe, the hood covering his head. In the small wagon, he seemed taller, thinner, and more sinister than ever.

Still, Solly was determined to be brave. Why did you kidnap that girl? You have to let her go, he was going to say.

But then the Ringmaster said calmly, "Are you here for another lesson, bo-oy?"

"N-no," Solly sputtered, still hacking from the dust.

"I think you are. Come. We will wa-alk Serena to her compound and then we will ta-alk." He reached out to lay a hand on Solly's shoulder.

"NO!" Solly flailed his arm. His fingers snagged the Ringmaster's hood. It slid back.

By the white glow of the console, Solly could clearly see the Ringmaster's face. He looked exactly like Freeble.

And once again, Solly screamed and ran for his life.

CHAPTER 18

Solly didn't see or hear the car bearing down on him until it was nearly too late. A horn blared. Tires screeched. A shrill voice yelled, "I-iii-diot!" But Solly registered those sounds only after he'd landed in a heap in the road under a streetlight.

Someone jumped out of the car and loomed over him. "What is *wrong* with you, Solly?" his stepmother screamed. "Do you want to get yourself killed?"

"Or dent your fender?" Solly muttered. He tried to stand, but Old Staircase shoved him back down.

"You'll move when I tell you to," she said, expertly feeling his arms and legs. "Nothing broken. Did you pass out?"

"No," said Solly. "Not this time."

Old Staircase didn't ask him what that meant. Instead she said, "Okay, you can get up now."

"Thanks." Solly rose. His butt hurt, but he didn't dare rub it. The last thing he wanted was Old Staircase examining his posterior.

"Why were you running in the road? And at this hour?" she demanded as they drove home.

"I'm being pursued by giant reptiles," Solly replied. If he hadn't been feeling somewhat gaga, he probably wouldn't have said it. He winced and held his breath.

"If you think you're funny, I suggest you take some clowning lessons."

"I have," Solly said. Quit while you're ahead, he warned himself. But he couldn't. "They said I'm a natural."

Old Staircase swerved the car over to the curb and stopped. "I've had it up to *here* with you, Solly, with those hangdog eyes and those smart-ass remarks. I'm not your mother. I'll *never* be your mother. The Beautiful, the Talented, the One and Only Dorianna, who could act, dance, sing, cook, keep house, and always look perfect. You and your father, you both hate me because I'm not her!"

To Solly's shock, she started to cry. Horrible snuffling sobs that sounded like a dog trying to bark and eat at the same time. He didn't know what to say or do. He didn't hate Old Staircase—at least not because she wasn't his mother—did he? He was sure she hated him because he wasn't, could never be, her son. As for his father, he never compared Old Staircase to Dorianna. He hardly ever *talked* about Dorianna. At least not around Solly. But he didn't much hug or kiss Casey, either—not the way he used to hug and kiss Solly's mother. And he never used to be away so much when Mom was here. Solly had thought maybe Dad wanted to get away from *him*. Now he wasn't so sure.

Suddenly Solly felt sorry for his stepmother. He didn't like her any better, but for a moment, he understood her.

Then, abruptly, she stopped crying and said, "I can see that keeping you from the circus isn't enough."

Solly's brief bout of sympathy vanished. "Not enough? Not enough?" You ungrateful boy. Scrub the tub and mow the dishes and wash the lawn . . . , he mimicked in his head. "Not enough to treat me like a . . . a . . . *servant!*" he blurted.

"That's exactly what I mean. I'm going to have to keep you inside, period. Until you shape up and stop acting like a menace to yourself and everyone else."

Solly understood what it meant to see red. "Keep me inside? What are you going to do? Lock me up with the crocodilians?" he rapped out, surprising his stepmother and himself even more.

"The *what?*"

"Why not just send me to Boldwangia so Dad and I can *both* get away from you!" He knew it was a nasty thing to say as soon as he'd said it. But he was too mad to care.

Old Staircase swung out and slapped him. She was sitting at an awkward angle behind the steering wheel, so the slap had little force. Still, it stung him into silence.

Fighting back tears, he said nothing the rest of the way home. He decided he'd never say anything to Old Staircase again. He'd become mute like some monks he once saw in a movie. If he found out who they were, maybe they'd let him join their order. Their robes looked kind of itchy, though.

When they reached the house, he started to shiver. The lizard was there. In his room. Waiting to turn him into an iguana. He tried to stop shaking so his stepmother wouldn't notice, but she did.

"You must be experiencing a little shock. You need some orange juice," she said briskly, throwing open the car door.

Solly opened his as well but didn't leave his seat.

He couldn't. He shivered harder. He could practically hear Freeble's voice.

"Maybe I should've taken you to the hospital," Old Staircase said, her voice uncertain with guilt and real concern.

He *could* hear Freeble's voice. *Do not be afraideeble. I'm here only to helpeeble you.*

Solly stared at his stepmother. It was obvious she heard nothing.

All at once, he stopped shivering. "No, it's okay. I'm fine," he said, getting out of the car and striding into the house toward his room.

He didn't get very far. Jason was blocking the hallway. He had a peculiar smile on his face.

Oh, no, Solly thought. I left him here alone. With Freeble.

"Greetings and salutations, you wonderful person, you!" Jason said, and threw his arms open wide.

"Hello to you, too, dear." Surprised, Old Staircase reached out tentatively to hug him.

But Jason brushed right past her and grabbed Solly in a bear hug. "Welcome home, buddy! I've missed you so much!"

Solly pulled away. What nasty little scheme was Jason working on now? Solly glowered at his stepbrother.

But Jason just smiled back. "My baby brother, my beloved boss, I'm here for you! Whatever you want, it's yours!" he announced.

Solly stared at his dazzled eyes and, to his amazement, he knew that Jason meant every single word he said.

CHAPTER 19

What did you do to Jason?" Solly asked.

The lizard shrugged, sitting calmly at Solly's desk as if it had just finished its homework.

It occurred to Solly that perhaps he ought to be more frightened than ever. After all, what could be scarier than a creature that had done something to turn his mad scientist stepbrother into an Igor? And Solly was sure Freeble *had* done something—even if the lizard denied it. But Solly wasn't afraid of Freeble any longer. Maybe it was the fact that Piggy was snoozing in the creature's lap. Maybe it was the crinkles at the corners of its yellow eyes. Whatever the reason, he was certain that the lizard was there to help him.

"Just a weeble switchereeble," Freeble said.

"A what?"

"A small hypnotic suggestion so the subjecteeble does the opposite of whatever bad behavioreeble he or she is used to doing."

Solly gawked at the creature. It was clear that Freeble was no longer a dumb kid. "Who *are* you?" he demanded.

"Freeble Komodeeble from the planeteeble Reptilia in the Chordata sector."

"Yes, but *who* are you?"

"Your faireeble godmother," Freeble said, with a toothy smile.

"My faireeble godmother? You're a *lady*?"

"Can't you telleeble?" Freeble replied.

Solly wasn't sure whether or not she was joking, and he decided it would be too rude to ask. Besides, he had more important questions. "What are you doing here? How did you get here? And why do you look like the Ringmaster?"

Freeble's stomach rumbled. She rubbed it. "I will telleeble you, but first . . ."

"Sneeble," said Solly.

"Yes, indeedy doody," said his faireeble godmother.

Solly fetched the jar of bugs he'd stored under his bed and handed it to her. She gobbled down about half of the contents. Solly sighed. He was going to have to go worming. Again. "Wait a minute—if you've got magic powers, why can't you make yourself some food?"

"Don't have that kind of magickeeble," Freeble said, the end of a caterpillar wiggling out of her mouth.

Ick, Solly almost said aloud. He turned his head till she finished her meal.

"Yumeeble!" Freeble sighed and let out one of her fragrant burps. "Now, what did you wanteeble to know? Oh, right. Question one: Why do I look like the Ringmaster? We are from the same planeteeble. Question two: How did I get here? I was broughteeble. Question three: What am I doing here? I am here to teacheeble you lizardry."

"To teach me what?"

"Lizardry. How to becomeeble a lizard."

"Why on earth would I want to do *that?*" Solly shouted.

"Is everything all right, Solly? Do you need help?" Jason called.

Solly groaned. His stepbrother was still sitting outside, guarding his bedroom door. Right where he'd left him. Where Old Staircase, or for that matter Mason, was, he didn't know or care. "Everything's fine," he called back.

"Are you sure?"

"Yes!" Solly barked.

"Okay, then, my dear brother!" Jason sang.

Solly rolled his eyes. "That's some hypnotic suggestion. How long does it last?" he asked.

"I don't knoweeble," said Freeble. "I've nevereeble used it before."

"You haven't?"

"No. This is my firsteeble assignment."

"Who assigned you?"

"I don't remembereeble."

Solly groaned again. It was just his luck that his fairy godmother would be an apprentice. "About that lizardry business . . ."

"It mighteeble come in handy."

"For what?"

Freeble looked blank. "Disguiseeble?" she said.

Solly could tell she was guessing.

"Disguise?" He shook his head. "It's a long time till Halloween. And I can't think of any other reason I would want to look like a liz—" He bit off his own words. His eyes went wide. He began to grin.

"You've thought of a reasoneeble," Freeble encouraged.

"Yes. Yes, I think I have." Solly laughed. "Bring out the mice and the pumpkin, Faireeble Godmother. Sollerella wants to go to the ball. Or should I say the *circus*!"

"Goodeeble!" said Freeble. She let out one more small burp and stood up. "Then it's time to begin."

CHAPTER 20

The thumping and yelling outside Solly's room woke him. He got up too fast and groaned. Between all of yesterday's running and the near collision with Old Staircase's car, he was sore all over. On top of that, Freeble's lessons had worn him out. Lizardry was hard work! Solly was good at arms and legs, but his head was another story. All those teeth to transform! But Freeble, asleep on the floor ("Out of my bed. You snore," he'd told her), promised he'd get it eventually.

"I *told* you—I want Solly to spot me. I need to practice my foul shots," Mason's loud voice thundered.

More like practicing *fouls*. Solly winced. He'd

played basketball with Mason a couple of times when his friends were too busy to join him. Some of the black-and-blue marks still hadn't quite disappeared.

"I told *you*—he's sleeping. You can't go in." Jason's higher tones drilled through the door.

"Jace, quit chaining my yank! This joke's getting old. You wouldn't let Mom in before, either."

Solly slid his feet gingerly to the floor. He vaguely recalled that Old Staircase had knocked on the door earlier, asking if he was feeling all right, and that he'd told her to go away. Jason must've seen to it that she did.

"She wasn't respecting our brother's wishes."

"Our *what*? Man, if I didn't know you better, I'd say you were outing flip!"

Then the doorknob rattled and there was more bumping and bellowing. Solly expected that at any moment Mason, who was a lot stronger than Jason, would come barreling into the room. But then Freeble awoke. She shook herself three times, spun in a circle first one way, then the other, dashed to the door, and dragged Mason inside.

"Dreeble cleeble geckoeeble," she chanted into Solly's stepbrother's face. Then she smacked him on the head and thrust him back outside the room.

During the silence that followed, Solly stared at

Freeble. It was one thing to know what his fairee-ble godmother could do—and another to see it done. Then he padded quietly to the door and put his ear to it.

He could hear Jason and Mason panting outside, sort of like tired Dobermans. Then Jason said, "You got it?"

"Yes," said Mason. "I got it. Our brother's wishes *must* be respected."

"I believe that's called a doubleeble whammy," said Freeble.

Solly hurried back to his bed, grabbed his pillow, and used it to smother his loud laughter.

"And now," said Freeble after a moment, "back to workeeble."

Lizards and humans have some things in common. They both eat, sleep, and play. But in most other ways, they're rather different—which was something Solly was learning. For one thing, they don't have the same sense of time. Four hours of Freeble's lessons passed much slower when he was Solly the person than when he was Solly the lizard.

The grumbling in his stomach finally made him notice it was time to eat. In fact, he'd been hungry for a while, but he'd ignored it. Now he couldn't ignore it any longer. Freeble was hungry, too. But then again, Freeble was always hungry. Was that

111

because she was a lizard or because she was Freeble? Solly wondered.

He didn't bother to ask. "Luncheeble break," he announced.

"Yum, yum," Freeble agreed.

Solly reached for his sneakers and tried to slip them on. They were way too tight. He looked down at his bare feet and saw long, long claws. "Oops. Forgot." He laughed.

"Never forget. Forgetting is dangereeble," said Freeble.

"Yeah, yeah, okay, so I goofed," said Solly, embarrassment and hunger making him irritable. Concentrating on his claws, he murmured, "Toeseeble, toeseeble," and watched them turn back into ten pink piggies. He shoved those into his Reeboks and walked out of his room.

His stepbrothers were standing at each side of the door. Jason had a shiner. Mason had a small cut on his chin. They both looked a bit ragged around the edges.

"Brother!" Mason saluted.

"Solomon the Wise!" greeted Jason, without a touch of sarcasm. "How are you this lovely afternoon?"

Solly nodded at them and tried not to giggle. "I am well, and you?" he responded.

"A bit ragged around the edges," said Jason. "But as long as you're safe and happy, it doesn't matter."

"That's good," said Solly, and he started down the stairs.

His stepbrothers followed.

"Uh, why don't you two stay here?" Solly told them. "I don't need your . . . uh . . . protection right now."

"All right," Mason said pleasantly. He and Jason turned and took up their places by Solly's bedroom door.

"Whoo," Solly whistled under his breath. His stepbrothers' behavior was funny, but it was creepy, too. Solly didn't like having guard dogs—especially when he wasn't sure how long they would stay tame.

Shaking off those worries, he hurried outside and began to search the tomato plants for more hornworms.

The plants were pretty well picked clean, so he started digging beneath them. Right away he found a fat white grub. Freeble's second-favorite treat, he thought. He held it over the jar he'd brought along, then paused. The grub looked tasty. Very tasty. Sweet and soft and delicious as a piece of marshmallow candy. Solly began to drool. He wiped his mouth with the back of his hand, popped the grub inside, and gulped. "Yumeeble!" he said, and began digging for more.

It was like the time he and his parents had gone strawberry picking. For every grub, worm, caterpillar, beetle he dropped in the jar, he ate two until at last he was full.

Just one more, he said, as he'd been telling himself for the past ten minutes. He'd found a cabbage looper he couldn't resist. Swallowing the caterpillar, he stood up, sighing contentedly. The sigh became a smile that grew wider and wider until it seemed to stretch his mouth, his head into a new but comfortable shape. He reached up and touched his face. It was cool and scaly and, he'd wager, green.

Yes! He'd done it! "Holy coweeble! It's so easy being greeneeble." He laughed and hugged himself. Freeble would be so pleased. But wait, *how* had he done it? Until he figured that out, Freeble wouldn't be pleased at all. *Dangereeble,* his faireeble godmother would say. He shook his head roughly, like a cartoon coyote who's been slugged with a hammer. It made him feel dizzy, but in a moment, his face returned to normal.

Picking up the bucket, he turned, wondering how many more hours he'd need to get his head on straight. Jason was standing there.

"How'd you do that?" he asked.

Solly twitched. He had a great urge to run up a wall.

"Do what?" he replied. He knew it was lame, but he didn't know what else to say. He could only hope that Freeble's spell would protect him from his stepbrother's nosiness.

No such luck. "You know," Jason said, "turn into a dinosaur."

"I didn't."

"You didn't?"

"Nope. I never turned into a dinosaur," Solly said truthfully. Dinosaurs were stupid. Lizards, on the other hand, had smarts. Or so he hoped. "All that staring into a microscope must be hurting your eyes." He mimed bending and squinting into the eyepiece.

"Oh," said Jason.

Whew, thought Solly. Then with a frown he asked, "Why are you out here? I told you to wait inside."

Jason looked apologetic. "You've got a phone call."

"I do? From who?"

"Didn't say," Jason said. "And I didn't want to pry."

There's a first, Solly thought. "Okay," he said, and marched indoors.

There were several phones throughout the house. Boldly he headed for the most private one— in Old Staircase's room. Closing the door in Jason's face, he picked up the receiver and said, "One moment, please . . . Hang up the other phone," he called to Jason. He waited until he heard the obedient click before continuing. "Hello. This is Solly."

"Hello, bo-oy," said the Ringmaster.

Solly nearly dropped the phone. "H-how did you know wh-where to call me?" he stammered.

"I kno-ow a lot about you, bo-oy."

The hairs on the back of Solly's neck stood up. He wondered if a lizard's scales did the same.

"We need to ta-alk."

"About what?"

"About your mo-other."

It was the last thing Solly expected the Ringmaster to say. "My *mother*? What's she got to do with this?"

"I will te-ell you. Tonight."

It was a trap. It had to be. The Ringmaster didn't know anything about Solly's mother, did he? He wanted to lure Solly to the circus and kidnap him, the way he'd kidnapped Serena. Or else make sure he never got to tell anybody else about the little girl. Solly's teeth started to chatter. He stopped them.

"If you know something about my mother, why

don't you tell me right now?" he said as coolly as he could.

"Tonight," the Ringmaster repeated. "At the circus. After the sho-ow. Will you be there, bo-oy?"

"I'll be there," Solly said. Silently he added, Except you're not gonna know it's me.

CHAPTER 21

"It's not fair," Mason whined during dinner.

"Unjust." Jason nodded in agreement.

"Solly should be coming with us."

"We've been through this already. Solly is being punished," said Old Staircase, her tone adding, What is *wrong* with both of you? You don't even *like* him.

"But why?" Mason persisted. "How can you punish Solly? He's a prince."

Solly choked on his tasty tuna jambalaya. Any other time, the sight of his stepbrothers sticking up for him would've tickled Solly immensely. But right now he was not amused. Not only was he wired from Freeble's rigorous lessons ("We will not stopeeble until you can changeeble at will," she'd said—and she'd meant it), but he was worried as well. Worried that Jason and Mason might actually convince their mother to let him go to the circus with them after all. And that was the last thing he wanted to do. He coughed loudly and irritatingly into the air.

It had the desired effect. "For heaven's sake, Solly, use a napkin," Old Staircase scolded. "A punishment is a punishment. It must be served."

"But what did he *do*?" Mason demanded.

Solly reached across the table and grabbed her napkin. How will she answer that one? he wondered and snorted. Loudly.

Old Staircase hesitated a moment before replying, "He was disrespectful and he tried to give away the gift . . . the toy I gave him."

"The toy? What toy?" asked Jason.

Solly peeked up from the napkin that was now childishly and (he hoped) annoyingly covering most of his face.

Old Staircase looked distinctly uncomfortable.

"That rubber lizard?" Jason scoffed. "You didn't even buy that thing. You found it in the basement. I saw you bring it upstairs the other day."

Solly gaped. Old Staircase found Freeble? Just where had he thought she'd gotten the lizard? In a store? No way. Through the mail? Ridiculous. He hadn't really thought about it at all!

"In the *basement*?" he said aloud. "*Where* in the basement?"

"What difference does that make?" his step-mother blustered. But Solly kept gazing steadily until she cut her eyes and admitted, "In a box your mother left for you."

Solly gasped. "My mother? My *mother* left me Fre ..." He caught himself just in time. "My mother left me that toy?"

"Yes, Dorianna left you that piece of junk you were so eager to give away."

Solly was breathing so hard, he felt as if he'd just run a mile. Did his mother think that Freeble was just a toy, too? Or did she ... how could she possibly know that the lizard was his faireeble godmother?

"Mother, you lied to Solly," Jason admonished.

Old Staircase drew herself erect. "I did not," she said. "And anyway, Solly was running on the road last evening. He nearly caused an accident. He talked back to me, too." She paused. Jason and Mason didn't look convinced.

His mother. Freeble. Lizardry. Circus Lunicus. Ringmaster. Serena. There's some puzzle here with a lot of pieces, Solly thought. He gazed at Old Staircase, knowing she certainly couldn't help him put them together.

She was squinting. Solly could practically hear her trying to come up with a capper—something to make her sons understand that Solly *had* to be punished. Suddenly her eyes opened wide in gleaming triumph. "And on top of all that, Solly is *not* going to the Circus Lunicus because the other night *he drove my car*!" she declared.

Oh, no. Wrong move. Solly gritted his teeth. He guessed what was coming. And he was right.

"No, he didn't," said Jason calmly. "I did."

"*What?*" Old Staircase shouted. "Then *you* can stay home tonight, too."

"*Oh, no!*" Solly yelled. "That's not fair ... I mean, he's lying ... It *was* me. *I* drove the car."

Old Staircase looked from one boy to the other, her face a mixture of puzzlement and disgust. "I don't know who's lying and who isn't. What I do know is that you're both grounded. Come on, Mason. We're going to the Circus Lunicus alone."

"But Mom, that's not ...."

"One more word and you can stay here, too, Mason," she warned.

"FAIR!" bawled Mason.

"That's it! I hope the *three* of you enjoy your evening at *home*." She rose, angrily banging her knee on the table leg, and limped out of the room.

Solly groaned. "Hurry after her and apologize," he told his stepbrothers. "There's still time."

"What for?" Jason said. "She was wrong and she knows it."

"Yeah, and if you're not going to the circus, neither are we," said Mason.

"But I *am* going to the circus!" Solly blurted, then clapped his hand over his mouth.

"You are? Cool!" said Mason.

"Tell us the plan," said Jason.

What have I done? Solly wondered. And what am I going to do now?

CHAPTER 22

Think. Thinkeeble. How did you get into my mom's hands?" Solly asked, pacing the floor of his room. Every few moments he'd stop and listen for the sound of Old Staircase's car engine. He didn't need to—Jason and Mason were on duty as lookouts.

"Searcheeble me," said Freeble.

Solly sighed. His faireeble godmother was no help at all. Who else lives on Reptilia? Freeble couldn't answer. Did Reptilians kidnap kids all the time, or was it just the Circus Lunicus that did? She couldn't say. How come the Ringmaster could make himself look human and she couldn't? She didn't know (though she suspected it had to do with her job).

Solly listened again. What was that? A garbage truck rumbling down the street. He ran his hands nervously through his springy hair. "Do you remember my mother at all? Pretty lady with green eyes and red hair?"

"Ladyeeble, no. Remember a little red-haired girleeble," Freeble replied thoughtfully.

Solly stopped pacing and stared at her. A little red-haired girleeble? Was it possible? Was Freeble supposed to be *Serena's* faireeble godmother? To teach her lizardry so she'd fit in with her kidnappers? Yes! That was it! No. No, it wasn't. It still didn't explain how Freeble got into the box Solly's mother had left for him.

Solly closed his eyes. He was trying not to yelp in frustration. Freeble shut hers, too, to recall why she was there. "I don't know who or what anybody is anymore," Solly said, snipping off each word. "I don't even know who *I* am. Solly the servant. Solly the lizard. Solly the clown. Solly the fool. I just know I've got to help that girl."

"Yes," Freeble replied quietly. "Help girleeble."

Vroom. From the garage below came the distant sound of a revving engine. Old Staircase was leaving at last.

"Solly!" Mason pounded on his door thirty seconds later. "The sail has shipped. The play's in ball. The *fird* has blown!"

"Quiet, *Huckleknead*," Jason shushed him loudly. "Solomon, it's time!"

"I've got to go." Solly's stomach fluttered. Freeble laid her hands gently on his head.

A wave of calm rippled through him.

"Yes, go. Help girleeble," Freeble repeated.

Solly turned and gazed into the lizard's imperturbable yellow eyes and nodded. As he walked away he heard Freeble say, "Help dooreeble?"

Another joke. This time he gave a short laugh. "I can manage the door myself," he said, flinging it open and falling into his stepbrothers' eager arms.

*   *   *

Solly and his stepbrothers could hear the audience's delighted cheers coming from the Big Top clear across the field.

"I wanna see the alligators. I hear they're awesome," said Mason, sounding more like age five than thirteen.

"How many times have I told you—we're not here to see the show," Solly explained. Fear was making him impatient. So much could go wrong with his plan, the first thing being that he didn't *have* a plan. Not a solid one, at least. All he knew was that he had to get rid of Jason and Mason while he made his way alone over to the gators. There were bound to be some circus folk near the wagons.

125

Solly's stepbrothers would stick out a mile there, while Solly (if all went well) would not.

"Tell us again what we're here for?" Jason requested.

"We're helping out a friend." Solly repeated the vague reason he'd given earlier.

This time, Jason wasn't satisfied with the answer. "What friend and just how will we be helping?" he asked. Solly was sure the hint of impatience in his voice didn't come from fear. Freeble's spell was wearing off. Solly could see the signs.

"You'll find out when the time's right," he asserted, as firmly as he could.

It had the right effect. "Of course, of course. It's your call—*always*." Jason backed off.

"Yeah. You're the boss," said Mason.

"That's right. I am." Solly hoped that statement, which he still didn't quite believe, would patch up whatever cracks were splintering Freeble's spell. "And don't you forget it!" He thought he heard Jason sniff, but it might have been the breeze rustling the leaves of a nearby stand of hickory trees.

Solly led his stepbrothers toward the midway. Maybe he should just tell them to play a few games of Blast the Astronaut and meet him by the rest rooms in fifteen minutes or so. But even if they still believed he was boss, he didn't think they'd go for that. They needed a task. They needed an adventure. Instead he switched direction and took them to the far side of the Big Top, where the performers came and went.

Behind the tent was a row of tall barrels, at least six or eight of them. They'd been there when Solly'd done his clown act. He had no idea what they contained. Beyond and at a right angle to the barrels was a crumbling stone wall, built by settlers many years ago. And beyond the wall were woods.

A huge burst of applause erupted from the tent. "Hide!" Solly commanded, scrambling over the wall. Jason and Mason didn't hesitate to join him. They had to crouch low, but Solly was just tall enough to peer over the stones at the tent's exit.

"Whoo, this is almost as much fun as scoring thirty-two points in a game!" said Mason.

"Shhh," warned Solly. "Watch."

Sure enough, a small troupe of acrobats pushed through the flap and headed straight for the barrels. One lifted a lid and dug his hands inside. The other three followed suit. Each scooped up something and swallowed it.

"They're eating," whispered Mason.

"Interesting," Jason murmured in a tone Solly didn't like. "Wonder what it is." He turned sideways to look at his stepbrother.

Solly had a pretty good idea, but he wasn't talking. "Shhh!" he repeated.

In a few moments the acrobats scampered off, turning cartwheels and flips. From the right came a shuffling and a low humming, like a choir seeking the right pitch.

"It's them! It's the gators!" Mason exclaimed as they toddled into view led by their trainer, with his two assistants bringing up the rear. Music blared from the tent. Clown music. The clowns were in between acts, helping the audience's mood and attention shift from jugglers to acrobats to alligators with ease. The audience's laughter rang out. Solly could picture the clowns—if their act was the same as he remembered it—racing, wriggling, bumbling around the ring, letting loose a herd of windup baby alligators, followed by a bunch of big inflatable ones they would wrestle, then sweeping out everything to make way for the star attraction.

Solly could almost see himself in a screaming yellow suit and a huge red nose, tussling with a phony reptile in the sawdust, throwing punches at it, and pretending to nail a fellow clown instead. His heart beat faster, the way it had when he finally got to face Zyphoid in the computer game. He shook his head. Dad's right. The Circus Lunicus is bad news. Help that girleeble and get away from here.

The gators were still humming, waiting for their signal. From the tent came another burst of applause and a blare of horns. The gators immediately stopped humming and started stamping their feet. The Ringmaster was about to announce their act.

The timing couldn't have been better. "Okay. Now listen," Solly said, quietly and urgently. "You two stand guard here. If the Ringmaster comes out, you have to stop him from heading that way." He pointed left. "Stop him any way you can. Got that?"

"Sure," said Mason, punching one fist into his other palm. "Any way we can."

"Right. I'll be back soon," said Solly. He was pretty sure the Ringmaster wouldn't leave the Big Top at all until the show was over, and he intended to be well away from there by then.

Giving his face a worried little pat, he took off toward the crocodilian enclosure, keeping as close to the ground and the shadows as he could.

As he'd expected, there were several folks coming, going, and hanging out near the wagons. They were all wearing hooded robes, and now Solly knew why. If it took a lot of energy to turn lizard, it had to take just as much, if not more, to turn human. Performing in altered form took even *more* energy. The lizards were saving theirs for the grand finale by reverting to their real form between acts. The

hoods were to prevent any stray humans from seeing them.

Oh, hell, Solly cursed. A hooded robe was the
one thing he'd forgotten about. Not that it would
have been easy to get one, even if he had remembered. But perhaps Freeble could have provided
one. Well, it was too late now. He'd have to make
the best of it. *Concentrate.* He could hear her
voice in his head. Faireeble godmothers must be
good at ESP. Obeying, he pictured green scales,
sharp teeth, long tail, agile feet. He imagined
grubs, worms, soft and succulent caterpillars. Yum.
Yumeeble. He felt his jaws stretch wide and his
cheeks grow cool and rough. He ran his tongue
over his pointy teeth. Perfect. And perfectly con-
trolled. He wished his faireeble godmother could
see him now. But walking through Mintzville, even
at night, with a six-foot-tall reptile in tow hadn't
seemed smart.

Relax, she tickled his brain. He didn't plan to
stay a lizard long, but he hoped it was long enough.
She hadn't told him how long the transformation
could last. Flies, beetles, stinkbugs, Solly thought to
steady his nerves. "Wish me luck," he murmured.
Good luck, he thought he heard Freeble say. He
scratched his scaly chin and strolled toward the alligators' compound.

He passed several lizards and nodded at them.

The crocodilian enclosure had a big alligator painted on it. Two roustabouts sat on the steps.

"Hi. What's neweeble, dy-bud?" one asked.

Oh, man, Freebleese, as Solly called it, and Backspeak. What a weird combination!

"The Ringmaster asked me to check on the girleeble," Solly replied, as calmly as he could.

"Girleeble?" said the other roustabout. Was that a hint of suspicion in his voice? Solly felt himself start to tremble. It made his face shift. *Be careful,* Freeble warned. Centipedes, millipedes, tomato hornworms . . . ahhh! That did the trick. "Serena," he said.

"She's in with the gatoreebles?" The second roustabout laughed.

"What did she do this timeeble? Try to flyeeble home?" said the other, also giggling.

"Something like that," said Solly, waiting for them to move and let him pass.

"You should put on your robeeble. In case any hairies wander here by mistake," said the first roustabout.

"Goodeeble idea," said Solly.

For a moment, nobody budged. Then, with some reluctance—whether from wariness or just plain laziness—the lizards moved aside to let him climb the short set of steps. He opened the door and went inside.

Whatever he'd expected, it wasn't this. The muddy, boggy smell he'd noticed in the Ringmaster's wagon was much stronger here, but the place was more homey. There were no bars, no cages. Just a narrow strip of firmer soil with spongy ground on either side and a couple of pools. The space was lit by moonlight not from the real moon, but from two artificial orbs that were set in a black ceiling full of glowing stars.

Amazing, Solly thought. He looked around. No circus folk seemed to be there. He expected they were all busy outside. His face melted and reformed. Human again, he yawned. He felt a little sleepy. Shaking himself, he called softly, "Serena?" There was a faint noise from the rear of the compound. Solly couldn't make out what it was. He walked forward slowly.

"Serena? It's me. The clown boy. I'm here to help."

The noise got louder. It sounded like a snore. He was nearly at the back of the compound now. The moonlight etched the design on a pair of cowboy boots resting by the edge of a darkly gleaming pool. "Serena?" he called, a third time.

Suddenly something rose from the pool. It was very large, very wet, and very fast. As it moved toward him rapidly, Solly realized it was the largest alligator he'd ever seen.

"Help me!" Solly yelped. He jumped back and tripped, falling hard on his lizard tail. *Forgetting is dangereeble,* he could hear Freeble say. He made the tail vanish. I'm lucky it didn't break off—though if it had, I guess I could always grow another one.

But there was no way he could ever grow another head. And as the alligator's jaws grazed his ear, he thought absurdly, Poor Freeble. Who's going to bring her sneeble now?

CHAPTER 23

The alligator began to sing in Solly's ear. It was the loveliest, most soothing song he'd ever heard. He thought he could make out the words. Or rather a *feeling* that turned into words when it reached the edge of his consciousness, the way water turns to bubbles when it wells up from an underground stream.

> *"Oh, Boy of Boys,*
> *Go on, be a joyster.*
> *If not here, then there.*
> *The world is your oyster."*

Solly sighed. They were ridiculous lyrics, totally nonsensical, but they made him terribly happy.

"Polly, is that a new song?" Serena came forward, stretching and yawning.

"Oh, Boy of Boys,
No sandstorms, no blizzards.
Daughters and sonsters
Are loved there as lizards."

"That's so pretty, Polly," Serena said, kneeling between Solly and the big gator and wrapping her arms around the reptile's neck.

"Swoony," said Solly. He was sitting on the ground already, but he let himself sink deeper into the soft grass as if his bones had turned to vanilla pudding.

Serena slid down beside him. "It's just like home."

"Just like," Solly agreed, closing his eyes.

Their shoulders were touching. Solly liked the sensation. It felt familiar, even though he certainly hadn't sat that way with her before.

"Oh, Boy of Boys,
Learn to be bolder.
Heart's in the eye
Of the beholder."

Solly's eyelids fluttered. He'd heard something like that once. But where? Oh, well, it didn't matter.

"Home is where the art is," Serena murmured, snuggling securely between Solly and Polly.

Solly's eyes sprang open. That was it! And it was the Ringmaster who'd said it. He sprang up with such vigor that Polly backed right into her pool, almost dragging Serena with her.

"This is *not* home!" Solly declared, grabbing the girl's leg.

"It isn't?"

"No, it isn't. It's what he . . . they . . . want you . . . us to think." He shook her foot. The cowboy boot came off in his hand.

"You're . . . you're . . . right. I want to go *home*. I want my mommy!" Serena cried.

"Yes, you do. And we're going to find her. Now!"

Solly tossed the boot to Serena. She slipped it on and scrambled to her feet. Solly seized her hand and pulled her toward the door.

Polly had gotten over her scare and was climbing out of the water hole.

"Oh, lonely child,
Sister or brother.
I'll be your friend.
I'll be your mother,"

she sang.

Serena let go of Solly and turned toward the alligator. Solly turned, too. The reptile's voice was drawing him back.

"No!" he yelled. "Serena, put your fingers in your ears and hum."

"Hum? Hum what?"

"Anything you want. 'Happy Birthday to You.' 'Row, Row, Row Your Boat.' 'Home on the Range.' Anything!"

"How about 'Everybody Loves Me, Nobody Hates Me, I'm Gonna Eat a Worm'?"

Jeez, thought Solly, how long has this kid been with the circus? "Fine. I'll hum that one, too," he said.

Fingers in their ears, humming away, he and Serena made it out the door.

They were in luck. The roustabouts were gone. But then Solly heard the singing and shuffling. Oh, no! The alligators' act had ended and they were returning to their compound.

"I'm gonna eat a worm!" Solly sang loudly, and turned into a lizard.

Serena gasped.

"Don't be scared. It's still me. And I'm going to help you."

"I'm not scared," Serena said.

"Good," Solly praised, though he was a bit surprised. "Now, walk! Don't run. Walk like we're doing exactly what we should be doing."

They sauntered toward the back of the Big Top—and the approaching alligators.

Please, please let us through, Solly begged silently.

"Had a nice visit with Polly?" the trainer asked Serena.

Solly poked her. "Yes," she said.

"Good," said the trainer, walking on. The crocodilian choir ignored them completely.

"Better put on your robe," said an assistant to Solly.

"Oh, right," he replied.

When they were far enough away from the pack, Solly thought quickly. Should they get Jason and Mason or just head out of the fairgrounds straight to . . . where? The police? He didn't dislike Sheriff Selig, but the man had no imagination. He wasn't likely to believe Serena had really been kidnapped by aliens. And if by some chance he did, he might get a bit too nosy and find out about Freeble.

Solly certainly couldn't bring Serena home, either. Old Staircase, once she returned from the circus, would call the cops, the FBI, the CIA—whoever—just to get on the news.

There was only one place Solly could think of that would be safe. Ruben's house. Carlos would help. And Grumpy. Grumpy had to know there was something weird about the Circus Lunicus besides their stinginess. As for Ruben, it was time to tell him the truth, and then maybe he and Solly could be friends again.

Yes. That was what they'd do. Go to Ruben's house. But what about Jason and Mason? It would be wiser just to leave them there at the circus. It would serve them right, too. Solly bobbed his head.

But then he shook it. Nope. He couldn't do it. Even if Freeble's spell was wearing off. Even if they deserved it, he couldn't just leave them waiting there to face the Ringmaster. He had to get them—all of them—out of there, and soon.

Solly transformed into himself. "This way," he urged Serena, loping toward the tent.

They were lucky again. Nobody stopped them. Some kind of march was blaring from the Big Top. What act was going on in there? Solly didn't plan to find out. His heart was thudding anxiously as he hoisted Serena over the wall and clambered after her.

"Jason, Mason," he hissed.

No one answered.

"Jason? Mason?" Still no reply. They weren't there. Solomon Yanish, you *are* a fool, he told himself. So much for doing the right thing.

"Who are Jason and Mason?" Serena asked.

"Nobody," Solly answered. "Come on." He started walking.

"But that's the wrong way," Serena said.

"We can walk on this side of the wall a little ways. It'll be safer," he explained quickly, taking her hand a bit more roughly this time. Something rustled in the woods. Probably a raccoon, he guessed.

"You said you'd get me home!" Serena complained.

"I will. But we have to get away from here."

"No, we have to get to the ship!" Serena's voice rose.

"Shhh! The ship? What ship?"

"You know. You saw it. Fafa doesn't think I can fly it, but I can. He can ride home with Memu or Botsie or someone else who has room . . ."

"What are you talking about? *What ship?* I didn't see any . . . Oh! Oh, lord!" Solly gasped. The Ringmaster's wagon. It wasn't a wagon at all. It really *was* a spaceship. Maybe *all* of the wagons were spaceships . . .

Somewhere to his right a twig snapped. "But why?" he asked, bewildered. "Why do you want to fly the ship? You said you want your mommy. You want to go home."

"That's just what I'd like to know, too," said Jason, stepping out of the woods.

Mason didn't step. He hurtled.

"Serena, run!" Solly said, shoving his stepbrother. Serena skittered over the wall as fast as a gecko.

Solly tried to follow her, but Mason had his arms pinned. "Tell us what's going on here, little brother," he said.

Then Freeble's voice commanded, *Transform-eeble*.

June bugs, Solly pictured—and instantly he became a lizard.

Mason let out a high-pitched scream and jumped back. "I knew it!" Jason exclaimed. "I knew he was a dinosaur! Maybe we could try a little experiment about extinction . . ."

"Extinguish yourself!" Solly yelled, and bolted over the wall, barreling through the open tent flap, past a pack of cavorting clowns, and straight into the center of the Big Top's single ring.

CHAPTER 24

The spotlight was blinding. For Solly that was just as well. Standing frozen in the glare, he was glad he couldn't see the audience. It was bad enough that he could hear them. "What a costume!" "Wow, it looks real!" They laughed and clapped at the boy-sized lizard. Then they began to complain.

"Isn't he going to do anything?" a little boy's voice piped up.

"Maybe I should arrest him for loitering," Sheriff Selig joked.

"Yeah, don't just stand there, Zardli Boy," Mason hooted. He was over by the tent flap Solly had entered.

"Great dino, rotten clown," Jason added.

"I paid good money for this?" another voice complained. Old Staircase, in the stands.

"He'd never cut it in my circus," Grumpy criticized.

Solly squinted through the glare. Was he hearing the voices in his ears or in his mind? He couldn't tell.

"DO something!" the little boy shrilled.

"Yeah," a chorus of voices grumbled.

I've got to get out of here. I've got to help Serena, he told himself. Jason and Mason were blocking an exit. There were two others. With enormous effort, he tore himself from the ring and ran for one of those. A cluster of clowns clogged his path. Waving oversized, spongy truncheons, bats, and boxing gloves, they advanced toward him, grinning wickedly.

The audience tittered. This was more like it.

"Help me," Solly squeaked, wheeling toward the third and final exit. No one heard him. No one but the Ringmaster, who stepped from the shadows, brandishing a lion tamer's chair and whip.

Solly tripped and fell flat.

The audience laughed louder.

"Help me," he repeated, crawling backward

until he reached the edge of the ring and could go no farther.

"Uh-oh. That clown's in trouble," he heard Ruben say, worried.

He lay there staring at the Ringmaster, who was towering over him, pressing the chair legs against his chest.

The Ringmaster stared back. *I'm giving you a chance, bo-oy*, his eyes, bright and fierce, seemed to say. *A chance to find out who you are, what you can be. It's up to you to ta-ake it or not.*

Freeble, what should I do? Solly asked silently.

Loud and clear, Freeble spoke in his head. *You knoweeble.*

I do? Solly took a deep breath. He could almost feel Freeble's hands on his shoulders, his head. And suddenly, he knew at that moment there was only one thing he could do: Make 'em laugh.

Quick as a lizard's tongue, he jumped up. He grabbed the Ringmaster's whip and cracked it on the floor. The Ringmaster winked and tossed him the chair. Solly caught it in midair. A cage suddenly appeared in the ring. Prowling and menacing just like the Ringmaster, Solly slowly began to back his opponent inside.

The audience rooted for him—especially when he turned on the clowns. Waddling, prancing, mincing, imitating each and every one, he drove them into the cage, too. His lizardy appearance only made the mimicry funnier. Dropping the whip and chair, he slammed the door, dusted his hands, blew a raspberry at his prisoners, and spun around to face the crowd. He threw up his arms like a pro wrestler, puffed out his chest, and swaggered around the ring. He boasted, bragged, hurrahed—all without saying a single word—and the spotlight followed his every move.

The audience whooped with laughter. Solly opened his arms wide as if to embrace them all. Then he thought, Well, why not? Why not embrace them for real? Clambering up the bleachers, he kissed an old woman, hugged a fat man, and stole a handful of his popcorn. He ruffled a little boy's hair, took his glasses, put them on, and teetered around the stands. He shook hands with a pole and leaned against a giggling teenage girl before giving back the boy's specs. Charging over to Old Staircase, he plopped himself in her lap, bouncing up and down like a baby, then he played with his imaginary pearls just the way she was doing.

Then someone yelled, "Uh-oh!" More voices joined in. "Look out!" "Catch them!" "They're getting away." Perching on the arm of his stepmother's chair, Solly struck a sailor pose and ahoyed the ring.

The clowns were sneaking out of the cage. The Ringmaster was already gone.

Shaking his fist, Solly began to scramble down the stands—and stopped at Sheriff Selig's seat. He whistled and gestured, "You! Come on!"

Getting into the spirit, the large policeman rose. Handcuffs dangled from his belt. Solly reached for them and managed to cuff himself to the cop. He jerked forward and backward as if the sheriff were tugging him. Even the sheriff was laughing. Slipping out of the cuffs, Solly led the haw-hawing sheriff down toward the ring. On the way, he rounded up the old woman, the fat man, the little boy, the teenage girl, and several other willing victims. Only Old Staircase refused to come.

Around the ring Solly chased the clowns until they disappeared, and he put his new prisoners from the audience into the cage in their place.

"I wanna be in prison, too," Mason boomed, barreling out from the sidelines. Solly was only too happy to oblige. Then he collared Jason and booted him inside with the others.

"More, more!" The audience stamped and hollered.

More? The cage was nearly full. And how could he top this act, anyway? Scanning the stands, his face split into a lizardy smile. Dashing up the bleachers one more time, he landed at the

Ramirezes' seats. A quick patty-cake with Grumpy, a pat on Carlos's back, a kiss for Ruben's mother, and then he turned with mock surprise to Ruben, greeting him as if he were a long-time-no-see old pal. Ruben laughed but only half played along until Solly took him by the hand. He started at the cool, scaly touch. Solly knew he was thinking what no one else had bothered to ask: Just what kind of costume *is* that?

"It's all right, Ruben. Trust me," he whispered.

Ruben's eyes opened wide. "What the . . . ," he gasped.

"*Trust* me," Solly repeated. "And come on."

For a moment it seemed that Ruben was going to knock him aside and flee. But then he nodded okay and followed Solly to the ring. Ruben headed for the cage, but Solly stopped him.

"Hoopla!" he whooped, throwing his arms in the air. Ruben blinked. "Go ahead," Solly whispered to his friend.

"Are you sure?"

"You bet I am."

"Okay. Hoopla!" Ruben echoed, and stretched out on the ground. "Hup!" He raised his legs.

To the audience's enormous delight, Solly was soon spinning around in the air, held aloft by his best friend's big, strong feet.

When they finished their act, the crowd went

wild. Solly and Ruben bowed and bowed, then threw open the cell doors.

The prisoners spilled out. The Ringmaster glided between Solly and Ruben, smiling and clapping. With a swell of pride, Solly looked up at him. "Welcome home, bo-oy," the Ringmaster said.

The words were even sweeter than Polly's song. They were not designed to lull him to sleep. They spoke to both his mind and his heart.

And he was terrified. The Ringmaster had won. Not through hypnosis or magic or anything Solly couldn't understand. He'd won by letting Solly's own wish come true.

Then all at once, whether from fear or fatigue or inexperience at transformation, Solly lost his lizardness. In the next moment a word from his last sixth-grade vocabulary test popped into his head: *bedlam*, meaning "a mad, riotous situation," meaning the Circus Lunicus had just gone totally nuts!

CHAPTER 25

Some people screamed and ran for the exits. Others screamed and rushed the arena. Still others sat rooted to their seats as if held there by Krazy Glue. "Ten-fifteen . . . no, ten-thirty-four . . . er, ten-seventy-eight . . . !" Sheriff Selig was shouting into a walkie-talkie. "Best damn act I've ever seen," Grumpy was roaring, slapping his thighs.

Piercing through the babble of frightened, astonished, excited, bewildered voices, like a siren cutting through a chorus of katydids, rose Old Staircase's sharp whine: "Solomon Yanish, I said you were grounded!"

Solly whirled in horror to see her hustling down the bleachers toward him.

Other folks were heading his way, too—Grumpy,

Ruben's parents, and Jason and Mason. But with all the other people coming, going, immobile, they were having trouble reaching him. The clowns and other circus folk tried to calm the mob. The Ringmaster called for order.

"Help! Ruben, help me!" Solly rasped.

But stunned by Solly's sudden change, Ruben stood frozen, his brown skin as pale as if he had frostbite.

Any moment now Solly expected to be crushed by the crowd, carried off by his stepbrothers, or withered on the spot by Old Staircase's furious glare. Instead something big and hairy clattered through the entrance that the Ringmaster had been guarding, parting the people as neatly as a policeman's horse. In fact, at first Solly thought it *was* a horse—perhaps a pony. Then he realized it was a gigantic and oddly familiar brown-and-white guinea pig. Riding atop its fat and furry shoulders was Serena.

"Get on!" she said. "It can hold all of us."

Solly shook Ruben. "Hurry!" he yelled, scrambling on the mammoth mount.

Still in a daze, Ruben managed to climb aboard. Serena dug her heels gently into the beast's sides and they galumphed out of the rear exit of the tent just as Old Staircase—and several dozen other people—reached the ring.

Outside, the air had gotten thick and steamy. There was probably a storm brewing. Solly found himself thinking he didn't want to get caught in it. I should go home before it breaks, he thought as they rode toward the wagons.

Home. The word made him laugh.

And laugh.

And laugh.

"Solly," Ruben said helplessly, squeezing his friend's forearms. "Solly, stop it."

"Solly, don't cry," Serena said.

"Cry?" Solly gasped. Well, his cheeks *were* wet. He smeared the tears. And suddenly he understood why Serena was trying to fly the wagon-ship. "Home is where the art is . . . But not when you're five . . . Home is your own bed . . . your own toys . . . Home is your own . . . mother . . . Isn't that true, Serena?"

Serena wasn't sure what he meant. But she said, "Sure."

"Solly, what are you talking about?" Ruben asked.

"Sometimes home isn't out here . . . ," Solly went on, gesturing around them. "Sometimes home is . . . up there." He pointed at the sky. "Right, Serena?"

This time she followed him. "Yes. Home is up there—even though we can't see it from here."

"Are you . . . You *are* saying . . . It's true, then?" Ruben said in a hushed voice. "The Circus Lunicus *is* from outer space?"

"Tell him," Solly said.

"Of course it is," she answered. She might as well have added, "Like, duh!"

"Oh, wow!" Ruben clutched at his hair.

Solly felt his own hair begin to stand on end. There was more of the truth to unravel, and it was giving him the shivers. "So, the Ringmaster never *made* you join the circus . . . ," he asked Serena carefully.

"Made me? Fafa wouldn't make me do anything. He and Mom asked me if I wanted to come and visit Earth and I said okay, but I don't like it here. It's not fun like home."

"Fafa?" Ruben said.

"Grandfather," Solly and Serena said simultaneously. Solly clapped his hand over his mouth. He hadn't realized he knew that until he said it.

"But he made you stay with Polly," he pursued.

"Well, yeah. But *anyone* who's in a bad mood has to stay with Polly. It's a circus rule. She makes you feel better. That's the alligators' job—to make everyone feel better."

"The alligators up there must be a lot different from the alligators down here," Ruben said, both awed and curious. "More like dogs."

"Our dogs back home aren't as nice as alligators. They curse a lot."

Ruben burst out laughing. But Solly twisted his head and frowned at him, so he zipped his lips.

They reached the wagons then. Solly slid off, followed by Ruben. Serena, clearly enjoying sitting high up on the guinea pig, didn't budge.

Something still didn't make sense, Solly knew. "If Fafa's your grandfather, why do you always look so . . . human?"

Serena furrowed her brow. "I don't know," she said.

"I doweeble," Freeble answered. She'd been standing right next to the Ringmaster's wagon, but Solly'd been so intent on talking to Serena, he hadn't even noticed.

"Freeble! How did you get here?" Solly exclaimed.

"I rode Piggy through towneeble." Freeble pointed at the guinea pig. "I made him biggereeble," she said, rather smugly.

"So I noticed," Solly said. They were getting close to the heart of the mystery, and Solly knew he needed to edge into it, the way he entered a cold pond carefully for the first swim of the summer. "Didn't anybody else?"

"Yes. But they thought we were an advertisementeeble for the circus."

"How long will he stay that size?"

"I don't knoweeble," Freeble said sheepishly.

"For a faireeble godmother, there's a lot you don't know," Solly said, his anxiety causing him to blame somebody. "And a lot you've forgotten."

"Yes, but I remembereeble most of it now. Do you want to know who you and Serena resembleeble?" Freeble asked gently.

"Yes," Solly said, lowering his voice.

"Dor."

"Door?"

"The girleeble whose faireeble godmother I was a long time ago. Dorianna. Your mother."

Solly breathed in so sharply, it sounded like a sob.

"She's his *sister*?" Ruben yelled.

"That boy's my *brother*?" Serena exclaimed at the same time.

"And Fafa—Fafa—," Solly stammered.

"Fafa's your grandfathereeble. Serena won't be able to transformeeble until she's eleven—same as you."

Of course. No wonder he'd wanted to help her so much—why he felt as though he knew her. Even though he hadn't even known his mother was going to have a baby. His mother. Something still didn't make sense . . . "But Mom always looked . . . normal," he said slowly.

"Because she is half humaneeble, isn't she,

Serena? Fafa is her fathereeble. Her mothereeble died when she was born."

The little girl nodded.

"She'd transformeeble when you and your dad were asleep, Solly. She never needed to changeeble as often as full Reptileeblians."

It took a beat before Solly dared to whisper, "*Is?*"

"Oh, yes. She was very sickeeble. She had to go home to get bettereeble—and she did. There's just one problemeeble . . ."

"She looks *exactly* like Freeble," Serena finished.

"What?" Solly blurted.

"Yes." Freeble nodded. "Your mothereeble is stuck looking just like a lizard."

CHAPTER 26

Polly and the alligators had their work cut out for them. Solly had never seen so many people in a bad mood, himself included. No wonder the Ringmaster had insisted that they gather in the crocodilian enclosure, with the fake twin moons beaming down on them and the gator choir humming away.

The gators didn't seem to be having the right effect on the Ringmaster, though. He didn't take well to being bawled out. His words were stretched out more than ever. "I kno-ow I should have to-old him right away," he was saying patiently. "But wasn't that yo-our jo-ob?"

"I was supposed to be hydrated within six

montheebles. Not six yeareebles later," Freeble answered back. The gators weren't working on her, either.

"It's not my fault his fa-ather never ga-ave him the bo-ox or that Dor couldn't return. I had to ma-ake sure he'd fit in."

"You weren't sureeble you wanted him to fit in."

"That's not true-ue." The Ringmaster's voice rose.

"You're still mad that your daughtereeble came to Earth for a one-yeareeble visit and ended up staying to marry a hairy and have babeebles," Freeble said, louder.

"*I* ma-arried a hairy, remember?"

"But she wenteeble to Reptilia with you and it was hardeeble for her there . . ."

"Make them stop fighting!" Serena said, upset.

Ruben giggled nervously. Piggy, back to normal size, squeaked in Freeble's lap. Only Old Staircase, Jason, and Mason seemed relaxed. And that was because the Ringmaster, who did indeed know a touch of magic, had cast a simple following spell to get them to the wagon, and Freeble had reworked her old obedience spell to get them to stay there.

"We love you, Solly," the twins crooned. "Don't we, Mom?"

"Speak for yourselves," Old Staircase retorted, but in the nicest possible way.

Solly couldn't take it anymore. "Shut up! All of you!" he yelled.

And they did. All of them. Even Polly and her chorus sank down quietly into their pools.

"Why?" Solly demanded, in a softer but quivering voice. "Why did my mother leave? Why did she leave *me*?"

The Ringmaster sighed. "She didn't wa-ant to leave you, bo-oy. She was going to have a ba-aby—your sister. But something had gone wro-ong. She got sicker and sicker. She knew if she didn't go ho-ome, she might die . . ."

"But she didn't tell me or Dad. She didn't tell anyone. She hurt us . . ."

"I think she meant to tell you bo-oth. She left Freeble to care for you in case she could not come ba-ack right away. Freeble was reprogrammed to tell you and your fa-ather what happened and even te-each you lizardry, if necessary. But the sickness affected her mind. She couldn't think of anything after a while but going ho-ome."

Solly couldn't begin to imagine what would've happened if his faireeble godmother had appeared when she was supposed to six years ago. His mother really couldn't have been thinking straight. But that didn't explain why the Ringmaster hadn't said anything. "She left with you, didn't she? *You* could have told us, back then before you flew away."

The Ringmaster didn't reply.

"You *were* mad at them," Serena piped up.

Startled, they all looked at her. For a little girl, she was very wise. Maybe kids grew up faster on Reptilia.

"I suppose I was," the Ringmaster said sadly. "But I also supposed that neither you nor your fa-ather wanted a lizard for a mo-other or a wife."

"You thought wrong!" Solly said angrily. But he knew that part of what the Ringmaster had said was true—Solly thought he would have loved his mother no matter what she looked like, but he wasn't sure about his dad.

"The great Dorianna is a lizard?" Old Staircase said, laughing. "Oh, my. Oh, my. I am sorry, Solly . . . truly, I am . . . But oh, my!"

Polly began singing again. Old Staircase yawned. "I wonder if she wears a lot of purple. It goes so well with green." She settled down again.

"We love you, Solly," Jason and Mason said once more.

"Oh, brother," groaned Ruben.

"You kept her from coming back to us, didn't you?" Solly, still angry, said to the Ringmaster.

"Oh, no! I would ne-ever have sto-opped her from returning. She was not we-ell enough to travel."

"But *you* were. Why didn't you come and get me?"

"The Collapsis."

"The what?" Solly demanded.

Freeble broke in. "Once every three hundred yeareebles, all routes to the Chordata system close down for a total of six yeareebles. Correcteeble?"

"Correcteeble," said the Ringmaster, with a faint smile. "That's why we couldn't come ba-ack."

"Meaning the Collapsis has just ended," said Solly.

"That's right. Your mo-other is well, but still not strong enough to tra-avel. She asked me to find out if I thought you were re-eady to return with us."

Everyone else in the room seemed to fade away. Solly held his grandfather's eyes. "And do you think I'm ready?" he asked, sounding both uncertain and defiant.

"I do, Solly," Fafa said softly. "The question is, do you?"

CHAPTER 27

Solly and Ruben sat on the steps of Fafa's wagon. Around them the circus folk—now their companions and friends—bustled about, taking down stalls, carrying gear, loading trailers. Solly was supposed to help, but Carlos offered to do it instead. Fafa agreed. He, too, understood that the two boys needed some time alone.

"It's been two weeks." Solly shook his head in amusement. "After what happened, I'm surprised they didn't run us out of town." Word of mouth about Solly's amazing transformation had spread faster than a field of crabgrass. But instead of Mintzville staying away, the townspeople came in droves. So did the citizens of neighboring burgs.

Solly's fame even reached the city. The Circus Lunicus had had to add a week of extra performances (including six matinees) to their scheduled run.

"Who'da figured?" Ruben agreed. He'd been part of the act at every performance, getting so good at acrobatics that Grumpy agreed to pay for six weeks of circus camp that summer.

"Even Serena stopped bellyaching about going home once Fafa let her ride Piggy every night," Solly said. It seemed that Freeble, too, had gotten good—at enlarging and shrinking guinea pigs. Solly and Ruben laughed.

Their laughter was real—and so was the sadness underneath it. The Circus Lunicus *was* going home—that very night—and Solly, who'd struggled those two weeks with all kinds of decisions, large and small, was going with them. The day before, the town even threw him a party. It was fun, but Solly's thoughts were somewhere else. What would it be like seeing his mother after so many years? It didn't matter that she'd look so different—after all, he'd gotten kind of used to Freeble—but would she be different *inside*? He hoped not.

"We'll be back next summer," he said, to make both Ruben and himself feel better.

"I know," Ruben replied quietly.

"Your dad said you could go on tour with us."

Ruben nodded and looked down at his hands. He didn't say that a year was a long time. He and Solly both knew that.

Solly looked down at his own hands. His nails were longer. He'd stopped biting them. His dad would be pleased—it was a habit of Solly's he'd always disliked.

Dad. Solly'd spoken to him twice since learning the truth about his mother. At first it was hard to convince his father that he wasn't lying, but at last he'd succeeded.

"I'll be on the next plane," Dad had sworn.

But he wasn't. Not on that plane or the one after or the one after that. He didn't even call for a whole week.

When at last he did, Solly was alone in the house, packing his things. He used to try staying out of Old Staircase and his stepbrothers' way; now they stayed out of his.

"What happened, Dad? You said you were coming home," Solly said.

"I know, son," his father answered, slowly, uncomfortably. "But you see . . . all these years . . . I thought . . . I was sure I'd gone crazy . . . Your mother . . . I saw . . . I *thought* I saw her as . . . as . . . a lizard. It turns out she really was one." Solly could hear the shudder in his voice. He realized now why his father had been so disturbed.

"But now you know you *weren't* crazy. Isn't that good?" he asked.

The question hung in the air. To his dismay, Solly realized that his father wasn't sure. Maybe he'd rather be crazy than have a wife and a son and a daughter he hadn't even known about, all of whom were lizards.

And then there was Old Staircase. "What about poor Casey?" Solly asked. He actually did feel sorry for her.

"She understands . . . ," Dad said. "I need time . . . to sort things out."

Solly didn't think Casey understood at all. He didn't, either. "Sort them out here!" he pleaded. "Come home!"

There was a pause, and then Dad said, "I'm sorry, but I can't. Not now. Not for a while." And he'd hung up.

Ruben seemed to sense what was on Solly's mind. "My dad says he's going to go to Boldwangia. He says if the mountain won't come here, then he'll just go and bring back the mountain . . . or something like that." He gave a little laugh.

Solly didn't laugh back. He was thinking.

A moment later Carlos joined them. "Everything's struck and ready to roll . . . or fly. Guess there's no need to drive the wagons out to the country. That's what they did, you know. They landed

164

these babies way out in a meadow where no one could see them, then drove them to the fairgrounds like regular old circus wagons."

Solly nodded. Serena had already told him that.

Carlos smiled. Then he cleared his throat. "I have a going away present for you. You know how sorry I am that I didn't tell you about your mom having disappeared. Your dad made me promise not to."

Solly nodded again. Carlos had been apologizing for two weeks now.

"She was gone when we got back to your house—I told you that. And I thought with the stress and all, your father had . . . well . . . gone loco, talking about lizards and all. And who could blame him, his wife disappearing like that. So I didn't think he'd want these—but I thought . . . I don't know why . . . that someday you might. They were all over the floor around your mother's bed." He held out a handful of creased papers.

Solly took them. *Home. Will return. Faireeble Godmother. Teach Solly,* said one of them. His mother had been trying to leave instructions.

He looked up at Carlos and beamed. "Thank you," he said, and brushed away a single tear.

"I have something for you," said Ruben. "You can work it into the act." He reached for the bag he'd brought along and pulled out Invisi-pet.

Solly laughed.

The wagon door opened then and Fafa looked out. "It's time to go," he said.

"Okay." Solly took a deep breath.

Fafa went back inside.

Solly and Ruben stood up. "Freeble's working on a way for me to send e-mail," Solly told him. "You might be the first 'hairy' to get a letter from another planet."

"Cool! But I don't want just words. I want pictures, too!"

"That might be expensive," Solly said. "And . . ."

"The Circus Lunicus is cheap!" he and Ruben finished together.

They laughed a little and then hugged each other.

Solly's eyes got prickly. He ran up the steps and entered the wagon.

"Mu-ufflers, Serena. To cut down on the noi-oise," Fafa instructed his granddaughter, who was helping him at the control panel. "And we don't need all those li-ights."

"But I like them," Serena replied. "Don't you, Solly?"

"Sure. A space-wagon's supposed to have lots of lights," Solly answered, brushing at his eyes.

"Uh-oh. You're ga-anging up on me," Fafa said, sounding surprisingly grandfatherly.

"We'd ne-ever do tha-at, would we?" Serena said, with a wicked imitation of the Ringmaster.

"Ne-ever," Solly said, with his own mock-solemn mimicry. This is how it would be from now on with his sister and not his stepbrothers—an "us" instead of a "them," a friend instead of two foes. Solly's already big heart grew a little larger.

Freeble piped up. She held out a bowl made of some pale purple metal Solly'd never seen before. In it were several tomato hornworms. "Sneeble?"

"Don't mind if I do," said Solly. He didn't ask where or how she'd gotten them. He just plucked up the biggest and fattest of the lot and swallowed it whole, smacking his lips loudly in satisfaction.

Serena eyed him critically. "I like tent caterpillars better," she said.

"Picky girleeble," said Freeble.

Solly grinned. What else would a circus girl like if not *tent* caterpillars? He laughed. I'll have to tell that one to Ruben . . .

Solly moved over to a small porthole at the side of the wagon. It glowed with a green light, and it had a shutter that could be opened and closed quickly. He knew it was the eye in the top hat. He gazed out and saw his best friend standing and watching. Carlos had his arm around his son's shoulders. My dad should be there, too. Solly sighed. Then the sigh changed into an exclamation. If the mountain wouldn't come to the spaceship . . .

"Fafa, we don't *have* to be home by tomorrow, do we?" he asked.

Solly's grandfather cocked his head. "Why? You do want to see your mo-other, don't you?"

"Very much! But we have time for one more stop on Earth, don't we?"

"Where on Earth?"

"Boldwangia," said Solly.

"Hmmm," said Fafa. "Yes, I think we could sto-op there."

"Good," Solly replied. "I've always wanted to see that place. Wherever it is."

He and Fafa smiled at each other.

"Here we go!" sang Serena.

Solly looked out the porthole again. "Hoopla!" he called softly, and winked the eye twice.

Ruben waved back excitedly.

Solly knew he was still waving as the space-wagon buzzed, blinked, and then vanished, winging its way to Boldwangia before it traveled on past a new moon and an old galaxy to the friendly swamps of home.